APOCALYPSE STILL

Stories

Leah Nicole Whitcomb

STARCLAY PUBLISHING

Contents

Apocalypse Still

The bags grow heavier after another night of restless sleep. Examining my neck in the mirror, I notice the bite marks have completely healed. I press against my jaw, under my chin, and around my trachea searching for any inflammation or softness. When I find none, I breathe a sigh of relief.

My closet is filled with turtlenecks of every color, fabric, and sleeve. I know it'll be hot today, but the office is always cold so I opt for a sleeveless turtleneck. Checking the mirror one last time before I grab my keys, I pull the turtleneck higher up on my neck and head out the door.

In the car, I search for *Apocalypse Still*—the podcast that tells the truth that the government is keeping from us. The latest episode was uploaded four hours ago. The host, Ryan, starts with his usual spiel about the government and the Infectious Disease Center. Apparently, the IDC said that they can no longer hope to contain the Zombies. As a result, Zombieism will be widespread.

Ryan adds, "There's this new phenomenon called Latent Zombieism. It happens when someone is bitten by a zombie, their bite heals, but six, eight months, hell even a year later, they turn into a Zombie. As always, the IDC is covering it up and saying that it's from a bite they haven't discovered, but we know the truth, folks. They're not telling us everything they know about Zombieism."

It's been almost seven months since I was bit. I slipped up once—thinking that I could enjoy an outdoor festival without a turtleneck. I was wrong.

"As always folks," Ryan continues, "keep wearing your turtlenecks to keep those bastards from biting you. And if you want more protection, check out my full body suits with anti-bite technology. Listeners get a fifteen percent discount with code *fuckzombies*. This is Ryan, keeping you informed and protected when the government doesn't want to. Signing off."

I pull into my parking spot at the office and rush inside. It's only been a month since we were forced to come back into the office. Almost everyone has been bitten by a Zombie, so the CEO didn't think we needed to be isolated anymore. I sit down at my cubicle and sanitize my desk before logging into my computer and checking my emails. As I'm scrolling, a guy three cubicles down sneezes. I jump and then spray disinfectant in the air. Teresa walks past mindlessly scratching her neck. She heads to the kitchen, pours a cup of coffee, adds creamer, sips, and then goes back to scratching her neck.

DJ and Shannon walk into the break room, so I grab my coffee cup from my drawer and join them.

"Hey Jenise. What's up?" DJ says. "Shannon was showing me her new dog."

Shannon turns her phone for me to see. It's a goldendoodle puppy. Tiny, like it's barely been weaned from its mother.

"Yeah, this sucker cost me three grand, but she's just so stinking cute that it was worth it," Shannon says.

I smile, nod, then fill my coffee cup. They talk some more about Shannon's dog, and DJ complains about his boyfriend not doing his own laundry while I sip my coffee. Teresa walks past the door again, still scratching her neck.

"Did y'all see that?" I whisper to DJ and Shannon. They huddle in a circle with me.

"No, what?" DJ asks.

"Teresa. She keeps scratching her neck. You don't think?" I stop and look over my shoulder. I don't want to say the word aloud.

"Noooo!" Shannon's eyes widen. "How can you think that?"

"It could be anything," DJ adds. "She could have a rash or rosacea. It's rude to assume things."

"No, no." I shake my head. I don't want to seem like a bigot by calling her a Zombie.

"She doesn't even have a bite mark," DJ whispers aggressively.

"It's just that I heard about this thing called Latent Zombieism where you don't turn into a Zombie until after the bite heals," I explain.

Shannon throws her hands up in the air. "You with your conspiracy theories. Come on Jenise. You're smarter than that."

"You know, people can't help that they've been bitten by Zombies," DJ says. "We've all been bitten by Zombies, and we're fine. My whole family's been bitten by Zombies, and they haven't turned into Zombies."

"Yeah, not everything is this huge conspiracy, Jenise," Shannon reiterates. "Latent Zombieism? What even is that? If the IDC says being bit is no big deal, it's no big deal. Let it go."

They walk around me, shaking their heads disapprovingly. As I return to my cubicle, Shannon talks with Teresa—even going so far as to place her hand on Teresa's arm when she laughs. Teresa looks distant, unfazed by all that Shannon's saying, like her mind is somewhere else.

"Howdy neighbor." Craig sneaks up beside me, and I jump. "Oh didn't mean to scare you. I was wondering if you could have that quarter two report to me before you leave."

"Yeah, the report." I shuffle through the stack of papers on my desk before I see the spreadsheet I need for that report and grab it. "Started on it. Almost finished," I inform him.

"Perfect!" He leans against my desk so he can face me and lowers his voice. "You know, Jenise, company policy states that you don't have to keep wearing turtlenecks. It's making a few people in the office uncomfortable." He raises his hands defensively. "I'm not saying you need to stop wearing them, but consider wearing them less."

"But it's for my health."

"Is it?" He squints his eyes. "People don't really get bit by Zombies anymore so there's no need to keep wearing them." His mouth widens into an empty smile. "Great having this talk with you!" He straightens himself and returns to his cubicle.

I tug at my turtleneck. Through glimpses of examining Teresa, I manage to finish Craig's report before I go home for the day. At an extended red light, I turn and see a couple walking down the sidewalk, holding hands. They move out of the way of something and keep walking. I lift from my seat to see over the car next to me and watch as a Zombie tears at the neck of a teenage boy. His carotid artery hangs in the Zombie's mouth, and blood spews everywhere. I look around at all the other drivers in the cars next to and behind me. Their eyes stay forward, avoiding the gaze of the Zombie. My heart thuds in my chest as I watch it chew deeper and deeper into the boy's neck until its last bite severs the head from the body. I had only heard of Zombies biting, maybe once or twice, not enough to decapitate someone.

It's getting worse.

A horn honks behind me knocking me out of my trance. The light's green. My hands tremble as I grip the wheel and speed home. I lock my door and sit in my bed until night falls. Once night comes, my eyelids grow heavy, but I toss and turn on my pillow trying to find a comfortable spot. As soon as I think sleep is near, my chest and throat tighten, lifting me out of the bed. My heart rattles around in my chest to the point that I can't breathe when laying down. I stack the pillows behind me to sit up and nod off for maybe a few hours here and there.

When my alarm rings, I drag myself to the bathroom mirror for my daily neck examination. I press against my jaw and cheek, checking for softness or inflammation. There is none. I press into my neck, and my finger slips into my skin. Pulling it back out, my neck rips open, exposing my thyroid and trachea. I lean into the mirror to examine my carotid artery. Upon closer inspection, there is no heartbeat.

Runaway

They took Mama away. It's been about a month since I last seen her. She left here kicking and screaming before they gave her the bit. The bit will shut anybody up.

My room was at the back of the house with Ms. Mary and Ms. Abigail. I waited til I heard them snoring and snuck out the back door, making sure to rub lard on the hinges so the creak won't wake nobody up. It was something Mama taught me when I snuck out to see her. I ran to the shack out back and walked in the doorway. Moving folk's hanging undergarments out the way, I made my way to the back corner to find Isaac lying half asleep, waiting for me.

"Lucy." His eyes blinked slow. He sat up on his elbow and let out a small smile.

"Isaac." I dropped to the dirt floor and laid beside him. The moonlight lit the ceiling blue. I held onto my fingers counting them one by one and trying to breathe slow and deep like Ms. Abigail taught me. Isaac sensed my worry.

"What you dream about? Before you came out here?" he asked.

Maybe he thought it was gone calm me down, but my dreams were nightmares. Always white men dragging Mama away leaving me alone, crying.

"I don't dream no more." A tear stung my eye.

"Not even during the day? You gotta hold onto something, Lucy. It's the only way we gone make it out."

He turned onto his back with one arm under his head and the other holding me.

"I dream about fishing. I went fishing once with my Pappy and Master Davis. Down at the lake. Ain't never seen a fish or water before. The water, it's something else. It has everything you need. We came back with a whole bucket of fish. Pappy told me they got fishermen. Men who just sit in boats on the water all day. Ain't gotta deal with digging ditches and planting crops. And you can feed yourself doing it. Make good money. Ain't gotta rely on nobody else to give you scraps. That's what I want to do. Bet it be quiet...and peaceful too."

He smiled thinking about it. "What you wanna do? If you could do anything?"

"It's silly." I shook my head.

"Ain't nothing silly. Tell me."

"I want a garden." I closed my eyes to see it in my head. "Not like here where we only grow food, but a pretty garden. I seen it in Missus Davis books. Flowers that were pink and yellow and purple. All these pretty colors. I want a house that is mine, and it's a pretty color, too. Maybe the house could be pink or yellow."

"Where you gone find some pink or yellow paint?"

"You told me to dream. I'm dreaming," I continued. "Anyway, in my yellow house I want to wear a big pretty dress, and I want to wear the perfume that make you smell like flowers and cake, and I want to put flowers in my hair and then when it's time for bed, I want to get into a tub and soak for as long as I want. And when I get out, Mama is there, and we sleep in a big ole bed with the drapes hanging from it. That's what I want."

"Why don't we get it?"

"Isaac!" I whispered and glanced around to make sure nobody was up and heard him. "You can't be talking like that."

"Why not?" he asked. "We can find your mama. You can have your house. I can fish."

"We could die." My heart thundered in my chest at the thought of it.

His hand cradled my face. "I wanna leave, and I want you to come with me. When the moon is black."

"Isaac." Fear flooded my eyes. I remembered the last person that tried to leave. Mr. John was dragged back by the dogs, his clothes ripped and blood crusted all over his body. Master Davis beat him for three days and left the welts to turn green and sour. "At least if we stay, we know we alive."

"This ain't no way to live."

My hand held his. His skin was as dark as the earth after a storm. Mama ain't coming back. Nobody that left ever did, and I couldn't find her sitting here. Isaac's plan was dangerous. Suicide. But living without Mama was a fate worse than death. I held his head. My fingers laid in the wool of his hair. Besides Mama, Isaac was the only peace I knew, and I couldn't lose them both.

"I'll go with you," I sighed, knowing that it may well be the last thing I do.

With his calloused fingers, he tilted my chin up to his and kissed me. "When the moon black, a'ight?"

I nodded and gazed up at the ceiling, watching the blue light shift to the corner of the shack. It was time to go back to my room. I dusted myself off, but Isaac grabbed my hand. "I love you, Lucy." He kissed my fingers.

"I love you, Isaac."

He squeezed my hand before letting me go. I retraced my steps back to the house, slowly opened the back door, and slipped into my room waiting for Ms. Abigail to wake me in the morning.

As small beams of sun poured into the room, Ms. Abigail shook me awake.

"I need you to go get me some eggs, baby," she said.

I yawned, grabbed a wicker basket, and went to the chicken coop. After gathering the day's eggs, I handed them to Ms. Mary in the cookhouse. Ms. Abigail strained the coffee, so I went to the main house to set the table for breakfast. Five plates, five sets of silverware, two coffee mugs, and five glasses for cider. Ms. Mary—still wet from having Adam—fed Master Thomas herself.

Master Davis was always the first one down. Then the kids, then Missus Davis. I carried their plates of biscuits, jam, and eggs from the cookhouse and set them on the table. When one of the kid's cup emptied, I filled it with more cider. As I walked past him, Mr. Davis gripped my thigh. My breath shook.

"Hand me my pamphlet, will you?" he asked.

I glanced at Missus Davis who wore her hatred on her face.

"Yes sir," I said, walking into the drawing room and grabbing *Who Shall Be President? The Hero of New Orleans, or John the Second, of the House of Braintree?*

Picking it up, my hands trembled. I breathed deep and returned to the dining room to hand the pamphlet to Master Davis who didn't look at me as I handed it to him. The scratch marks peeking from under his collar were a faint pink. Mostly healed.

"Lucy, I need you to ready the children and then come up to my room. We're going to town this morning," Missus Davis said, staring at Master Davis who wouldn't take his eyes off his pamphlet.

He let out a "hmm" with the smoke from his pipe. After I bathed and readied the children, I went to Missus Davis's room. She sat in front of the vanity, removing the rags from her hair.

"Let me help you Missus Davis," I reached for the next rag, gently pulling it away to reveal the curls. When I finished, she handed me the brush to lightly brush the curls out. I took care with her hair, holding it the way I wished someone held mine. When it was brushed to her liking, I pinned the front back and away from her face. While I did her hair, she stared at me in the vanity. She waited til I finished before shaking her head.

"You're lucky my husband's a good man."

I stared at her reflection in the mirror, unsure of her meaning.

"If you were at any other farm or God forbid, a plantation, they would've shipped your mama off as soon as you could walk. You lucky he let her stay around as long as he did."

"I know, ma'am." I swallowed the hard mass in my throat.

"And what an ungrateful whore she was. Clawing at him like that? She's lucky he didn't kill her." She walked over to the partition. "Help me into my dress."

I wiped my dampened eye, cleared my throat, and followed her to tighten her corset and tug her day gown over her head. I pulled her hair from out the back of the dress and let it fall on her shoulders. She wiped the front of the dress before her fingers got stuck in a hole. "Get the needle and thread."

Grabbing the sewing kit, I kneeled next to her and licked the thread before pulling it through the eye. I started at one end of the hole and worked towards the other making sure to pull the gown away from her thigh. Maybe I didn't pull it far enough because she slapped me. "Ow! Be more careful."

My cheek stung, but I replied, "Yes ma'am."

I finished her dress, and when she left with the kids, we all breathed a sigh of relief. The house was clean. The laundry was washed, dried, and put away. Ms. Mary knitted in the rocking chair of the drawing room while I looked out the window. Master Davis held his journal and supervised the hands outside. Isaac hoed, preparing the soil for planting season. I must've looked at him with too much longing because Ms. Abigail warned, "Don't let Master Davis see you like that. He be quick to ship that boy off. Whatever bit of happiness you got, you gotta keep it away from them."

"Yes ma'am."

She cupped my face, stared into my eyes, and sighed. The wrinkles deepened around her soft brown eyes. "You still a baby yourself. I remember when your mama was brought here holding your little hand. You could barely walk, poor thing. That was what? 'Bout twelve, thirteen years ago." She shook her head. "You just a baby." Her hands met mine, and she rubbed her thumbs over the backs of them. "Your nerves still shot?"

"A little," I admitted. Nothing could stop the trembling.

"Remember what I taught you. Breathe with each finger. One—" She held my pointer finger and breathed in slow and deep.

"Two—" She grabbed my middle finger and did the same. "Remember, you gone make it through this. Trouble don't last always."

"Thank you, Ms. Abigail,"

"Of course, baby." She smiled softly before sitting down.

***

The next night Isaac told me the plan: We leave at our usual meeting time and find a river. Rivers had everything we needed to survive. Once we make camp, we find Mama. Then, we follow the stars to freedom. My nerves got worse and worse as the days passed. My chest seized up in the middle of the night; it felt like I was dying. It was nine days from the time Isaac said we run away to the time the moon disappeared from the sky. When the moon blackened, I grabbed my small bag of food and jar of cider, wrapped a mojo bag around my thigh, rubbed lard on the door hinges, and slipped out to meet Isaac. He waited for me at the edge of the forest with a machete he took from Master Davis.

"Ready?" His other hand waited for mine.

"Ready," I said, placing my hand in his, and we walked into the woods together.

The leaves crunched under our feet. We used walking sticks to guide us. Most of the path was clear, but in some places the limbs and vines twisted together making it impassable. Isaac chopped through the dense growth and eventually we found a trail, probably worn down by Indians. We walked next to it, hiding behind the trees so we wouldn't be caught.

After an hour or so of walking, we heard horse hooves. Isaac grabbed my shoulder and pulled me low to the ground. We crouched waiting for the horse to pass. Once it did, we kept walking, traveling until sunlight dotted the horizon then we rested. Isaac let me sleep first, and when I woke up, he went to sleep.

Ever since we left, I thought my nerves would worsen, but I hardly noticed the tremble in my hands or the fear rolling around in my chest. It'd been years since I spent the day outside so I closed my eyes, laid my head against the ground, and listened to the wind whistle through the trees. The birds chattered and hopped along the branches, and the sun kissed my cheeks. I grabbed the leaves by my side and rubbed its sandy rough texture between my fingers. For the first time in my life I felt warm and wrapped in light. Was this what freedom felt like?

When Isaac woke up, we waited til the sun began to set in the west before we walked again. Once the moon was high in the sky, we heard the roar of water.

"I think we're almost there," Isaac said.

We walked faster toward the roaring, so fast we almost didn't hear the horse hooves and dogs barking behind us. We ran towards the hunting cabin a little ways off. Isaac pressed me against the wall, holding his hand over my mouth. The dogs got closer, barking only feet away.

"We know you in there," one of the pattyrollers said.

"Take this," Isaac whispered, reaching behind him and pulling a pistol out of his britches.

"Where'd you get this?" I asked, but his hand muffed my words.

"I'll go back. You run."

My eyes widened, and he let his hand down from my mouth. He nodded toward the window for me to go through there while he turned himself in.

I grabbed his sleeve. "You can't leave me."

"Go," he said, his voice firm. "Find your mama."

A tear fell down my cheek. My hands shook again, but this time my heart broke out into a chorus. He opened the door and put his hands up walking toward the two men on horses.

How much more they gone take from me? How much longer I gotta count my fingers and breathe through it? How much more surviving but never living? I moved into the doorway, aimed my best at the head of the man on the left and shot. A second later a red hole appeared where his eye used to be. His horse reared back, jerking his body off, before running into the woods. The dogs whimpered and scattered as the other man fumbled to get his gun, but his horse—spooked from the shot—knocked him off, too. Isaac snatched his machete from the ground and chopped at the other man's neck until blood poured out of the gash. We watched their bodies writhe on the ground, trying to hold onto the last bit of life they had left.

They ain't taking nobody from me ever again

Superhuman

Jon struggles under the weight of the plane as it nosedives to the ground. We were dispatched because an electrical fire spread, and the pilots needed help landing one hundred and fifty eight passengers safely. Right now, smoke emanates from the back wing; passengers are screaming; and we have to figure out where to land this plane without causing major property damage. Scanning the horizon, I see the Mississippi River which means we're probably above Vicksburg now.

I grab the tail end of the plane and growl while pulling it towards me. My biceps are taut as I take the weight off of Jon's shoulders.

"Magnificence!" I call his code name. "We can land past the river."

The passengers won't get to New Orleans as they planned, but we can get them to Louisiana.

He turns his head to check and then yells back. "Got it, Ala! Incoming! Four o'clock!"

Still grabbing hold of the plane, I turn to see the figure flying towards us: Chris. In plainclothes, no less.

"Nao—I mean, Ala. Mayor Grambling wants to see you."

"Now?! Doesn't he know I'm a little busy?"

"He says it's urgent. I'm here to replace you."

I groan, letting go of the plane. Jon grunts from the sudden weight shifted onto his body, and Chris grabs the end of the plane taking my place.

"Land it over there. Past the river," I instruct before I fly back to base to change into my plainclothes.

Walking down the sidewalk, I kick a stray pebble. He does this every time. As soon as I'm knee-deep in a mission, the mayor has some "important business" he needs to discuss. I glance up at the cerulean blue sky and forcefully exhale. I should be up there fighting crime, making a difference in the world, not down here grounded—in every sense of the word.

Turning onto my street, I notice that there's a new flyer stapled to the telephone pole. My heart drops when I see the picture. It's another missing Black kid. Her name is Azeayah. She's wearing glasses, smiling. Her hair is divided into two afro puffs with bows decorating them. She's only eight years old. I shake my head and take a flyer, folding it into a tiny square before sliding it into my back pocket. That's the fourth kid this month.

The garage door is open when I get home. Dad's head is under the hood of his 1967 Chevy Impala. It seems like more of an ornament at this point because he's been working on it since I was little but has not driven it once .

I sigh loud enough for him to hear me. He jumps, startled, then wipes the oil off of his hand.

"Naomi, you're back."

"Yes, because *Mayor Grambling* wanted me on a *Saturday* when I'm *working*."

He leans back against the car's bumper. "You didn't have breakfast with me this morning."

I lean my head back and groan. "Dad!"

"Fine! Fine," he relinquishes, his palms in the air. "A burning plane? Do you know how dangerous that is? Why couldn't you get a cat out of a tree? Help an old lady move a couch? I don't know, something less dangerous."

"Dad," I sigh.

"It's just that if you worked in my office, you could—"

"Dad!" Not this again. *Naomi, get a real job with a 401K where you don't have to use an alias and can get a regular paycheck.* How many times is he gonna give this speech?

"It's a stable job where you can make a difference. I don't see why—" He quiets then stares past my shoulder. It's Captain Oglesby. Dad turns his attention back to me. "We'll talk about this later."

He wipes his hands some more and plasters on a smile before walking down the driveway. "Captain Oglesby!"

"Mayor."

I walk through the garage and into the house. Inside, my shoe sticks to the linoleum. There's reddish-brown footprints all over the floor. I check my soles and sure enough, it's covered in sticky oil. I exhale then hover over the floor, pressing my ear to the door. Dad and the Captain speak in hushed tones, but I can clearly hear the name: Luke Olsen. And then there are fragments: missing, superhuman suspected, retaliation, monkeys? Dad gives his fake tight chuckle for when he wants to come off as non-threatening while seething underneath. Then there's footsteps receding, and Dad muttering, "Jackass."

I fly to my room and pull out my journal that I've been using to track these disappearances. Luke Olsen is part of the group NARA (National Association for Real Americans). They've been around for decades—solidifying their cause in the summer of 2020 when they violently overtook many American cities reclaiming them for "real" Americans: white able-bodied men. Olsen is one of four men I've found in our town who are connected to the group. The others are Harry Gables, Chad Bailor, and Daniel Friedelson. Although they don't publicly declare their affiliation with NARA, they all have the same othala rune tattoo on their left forearms. It's an Anglo-Saxon character that white supremacists co-opted at the beginning of the twenty-first century.

Jon and I have been building a case on them over the past year when the first Black child went missing—eleven year old Taymar. At first, it was a child missing once every other month, but now it's escalated to four missing children this month. I pull the flyer out of my back pocket and add it to the packet of papers at the back of my journal. So far, every child that has gone missing has eventually been found dead.

We suspect NARA is behind it because Black people have been their public enemy number one since December 2020. During the Great Conjunction of 2020, Saturn and Jupiter aligned for the first time in almost four hundred years. It was at that time, we got our superpowers. Why only Black people? Some say it's genetic. Others claim it's a cosmic gift. Some credit the work of Black women who could conjure the powers of the universe and shared those powers with other Black people. Who knows? But since 2020, all Black people are assumed to be superhuman.

Assumed, but powers don't always show up, especially in racially mixed people. That doesn't stop people of other races from trying to have babies with Black people in the hopes that their child will be a superhuman. For the Black people who do have powers though, we all have super strength as a base power. Most of us have another power, like me and Jon can fly. Dad has super speed, and I know others who can teleport, have super hearing, or are bulletproof.

That first year, everyone got their powers instantly. I was three so I've only known a life with superpowers. We don't know why, but after that year, it seems that Black children's powers don't activate until they're around twelve. In rare instances—usually when the child grew up in a hostile environment—they would get their powers earlier. This is why it's so concerning that Black children are going missing before they get their powers. They can't even defend themselves.

Still, if what I overheard is true, a superhuman may have taken Olsen and who knows what they're going to do with them. Jon and I have tried our best to keep this under wraps. I've even kept physical research to ensure that neither the government digitally spies on us nor that a superhuman hacker finds our research and tries to retaliate. But somehow, a superhuman knows Olsen is involved and may be holding him hostage. If that's the case, it'll ruin the case we're trying to build. Dad is always like, *Let the justice system handle it*, but many judges will throw out a case because of "superhuman interference." Especially Judge Alex, who's been spotted with Friedelson and may be part of NARA himself. If our case isn't irrefutable, there's no justice for the seven kids who've been murdered and the three now missing.

I lay down on my bed, drag my hand over my face, and exhale. This shit is hard.

Dad knocks on the door, so I shove my journal under my mattress before telling him to come in. He opens the door and waves a bottle of brandy in the air.

"I know it's early,"—it's a little after one in the afternoon—"but I could tell that we both needed a little pick-me-up."

He sits beside me on the bed and pours some brandy in a cup then hands it to me. I sip it, letting the sweet apricot flavor wash over my mouth before I swallow. A burn lights up my throat and chest. I swirl the amber liquid in the glass before sipping again and sighing.

Dad drinks the entire drink in one gulp and pours some more. "I know you think I'm being hard on you, but they didn't have this superhero stuff when I was your age. It was just comic books, not a real job."

Superhumans are not required to work as superheroes, but we can "use our talents to serve the American government" as the recruitment posters put it. And we get paid, not as comfortably as other government workers, like Dad, but it's something.

"I know, Dad."

"It's just—" he pauses, studying the cocktail glass. "It's dangerous out there, and I'd never forgive myself if something happened to you."

"I can take care of myself." I remind him.

"I know you can, but I don't trust the world around you."

"I understand, but I have Jon. We watch each other's backs."

He scoffs, "Wonder Boy."

"Magnificence."

"Same difference."

At an impasse, we sip our drinks in silence before Dad tries again.

"I want you to work with me." He raises his hand to silence my impending protest. "Hear me out. When I was growing up, I never thought I'd be mayor of this town. We never had a Black mayor. Hell, we barely had Black teachers in schools. There were a few of us working as policemen and firemen, but we rarely saw ourselves in positions of authority. My parents worked multiple jobs, never getting paid enough and always being tired. I didn't want that for myself, and I don't want that for you."

"I get it, though," he continues. "You want to be a hero. You want to make a difference, but we make a difference for hundreds of children in my office, and it's a lot *safer* than what you're doing now. Naomi, you're all I have."

"Dad," I cover my eyes with my palms and exhale. "Why do we have these powers if we aren't meant to use them? Right now, there's another girl missing: Az—"

"—Azeayah Walker." His jaw tightens before he clears his throat. "I know. I remember the names of every single child that disappeared and turned up dead."

I watch him as he turns the cocktail glass in his hand.

"You're too young to remember how bad the world used to be. You've been a superhuman damn near your whole life, but when I was a little boy, every day you'd turn on the news and another Black person would be murdered. By police. Shot in their sleep. Unarmed. Defenseless. And it'd be children, too. I didn't think I'd make it to eighteen."

A tear drops from the corner of his eye and rolls down his cheek.

"Then in 2020, that zombie virus spread, and NARA murdered Black people left and right while burning down all those cities. We went through hell to survive so I thought our powers were a gift. We could finally defend ourselves, and for the most part, the killings stopped. I think they were afraid of us." He scoffed. "I doubt I'd be mayor if half the town weren't scared of me and what they *think* I'm capable of. But now? Now, the children are dying again, and I know you are powerful, Naomi, but you are not invincible. None of us are."

He throws his head back to finish the last of his drink before standing and walking to the door. "Please, think about my offer."

When he leaves, I bury my face into the pillow and groan. I know Dad wants the best for me, but I can't in good conscience take a safe, cush job when kids are being abducted and murdered. I can't turn a blind eye to it, and yes, maybe Dad isn't turning a blind eye either, but I don't know. I don't know what to do.

The rhythmic tap on my window as I'm falling asleep tells me it's Jon. I raise it to see him hovering above the ground.

"What's wrong?" I ask. Him showing up this late can rarely be good news.

"It's Olsen," Jon whispers.

I rub my eyes remembering Dad's earlier conversation with Captain Oglesby. "He's missing."

"He's dead."

Fuck.

I drag my hand over my mouth and shake my head.

"That's not all," Jon says. "He was dismembered. Police only found his head and tattooed arm. They don't know where the rest of him is."

I cross my arms and exhale sharply. "They think it's a super-human, don't they?"

He nods.

"Jon, what are we going to do? The judge will never take our case seriously and those kids—"

"—Bailor's missing."

"No," I shake my head. "Jon, no."

"Are you sure no one's found our research?"

"No. I don't know how that could be possible...unless someone broke into our house and knew to check my room, but who would break into the Mayor's house?"

I pace in front of the window. "Maybe another superhuman or a group of superhumans are also investigating this. You can't just snatch a bunch of kids, and no one notices. Maybe they have the same names, but they're going after NARA."

"Vigilante justice."

The words stop me in my tracks as I gaze at Jon. The street light shows only a glimpse of his taut face.

Vigilantes. They meet violence with more violence when there are other ways. I understand that denied justice can be frustrating, but superhumans stooping to NARA's level makes them just as bad as NARA. We can rise above the violence. We can be better than them. But the question remains is how are we going to do that when kids keep getting murdered, and we're running out of ways to save them?

I sit at the edge of my bed and tuck my head in my hands. "Jon, what are we gonna do?"

"Maybe we condemn the vigilante? Call them a rogue agent or something?" he offers

"What if they want us to bring in the vigilante?"

Jon sighs. "Let's hope it doesn't come to that, but I'll keep you posted if I hear anything else."

He flies off. I close my window, crawl back into bed, pull my knees into my chest, and struggle to fall asleep.

Dad playing his oldies in the garage wakes me the next morning. Rubbing my eyes and yawning, I stumble to the kitchen and find pancakes on the stove. I squirt some maple syrup on one and roll it up before biting into it. The news is muted so I read the headlines while eating my pancake roll-up. There's theft, suspected superhuman activity, and the weather before a breaking news alert takes over the screen. Luke Olsen's picture sits in the right corner. His face is solemn with his beady eyes and jet black hair. I turn up the volume to hear over Dad's 2000s music.

"—body of Luke Olsen has been found in the quarry," the newscaster reports. "Police suspect superhuman foul play. Olsen's known associate Chad Bailor has also been reported missing, and police are looking for any information you may have about his whereabouts. Please call—"

As I click the mute button, I hear a scream. It's muffled under the sound of the music so it takes me a while before I realize Dad could be hurt. I fly to the garage door and take it off its hinges. In a flash, I see Dad holding a severed white arm with an othala rune tattoo that drops into a steel drum and shoves the barrel against the wall. He turns to me, shocked, with his dark apron drenched in blood.

"Dad?"

Entangled

"It's yours if you want it," he says.

His blue-gray eyes stare directly into me. Dark scruffy stubble lines his chiseled jaw. I scramble for a response, but his deep voice conjures butterflies in my throat that I struggle to swallow down. He extends the red apple to me, wanting me to take it.

"Thanks." I place it on the tray.

"I'm Caleb by the way," he says.

"Shauna."

"Aren't you in Professor Tracy's 11 AM? Calculus?"

"Nope." I pick up my tray and turn towards him as the students shuffle around us. "Wrong person."

"Weird." He scrunches his face. "I could've sworn I've seen someone as beautiful as you before."

I can't help but giggle. "Smooth."

"I thought so." He smiles, picks his tray up, and walks backwards away from me saying, "Well I'll see you around."

My cheeks burn as my mouth curves into a smile. I walk to the table against the wall where Bijal waits for me.

"Shauna?" She watches me sit down, her mouth agape. "Were you talking to *the* Caleb Williard?"

"How you know his government name like that?"

"He's like, top ten hottest guys on campus." She looks past my shoulder to the table where he sits.

"I've literally never seen him before." I use my fork to stir the rice on my plate.

"That's because you are holed up in the math department all the time. You gotta go out. Live a little." She stuffs a forkful of salad in her mouth.

"Sorry, but some of us came to college to get a degree."

"That doesn't mean you can't have a little fun while you're at it." She points her fork to me and winks.

I sigh. "He said I was beautiful."

"Ahhh!" she squeals, clapping her hands excitedly.

"No Bijal. That's corny."

"It's cute."

"It's—" My phone buzzes in my pocket. I fish it out and find a DM from freebigwilly98: *Hey*

The boy works fast.

***

"I'm happy you took me up on my offer," Caleb says, looking up from his menu.

"Well, I can't turn down the opportunity to not eat cafeteria food."

He laughs. I shift in the dress I borrowed from Bijal, the bodycon dress she insisted I wear because mine were "too churchy." Looking around at the other people here, it seems like she was right. The tables are draped in tablecloth. Each booth's lit by a low hanging light and an accompanying candle in the middle of the table. Pothos and Chinese evergreen plants hang from planters attached to the walls. If this wasn't a first date, I'd be pretty sure it was a proposal dinner.

"Why did you slide in my DMs and ask me out?" I have to know why one of Bijal's "hottest guys" wants to go on a date with me.

"I know what I want." He stares directly into my eyes, and my heart beats in my ears. "And I don't know, I thought I met you before, like we had Calculus together or—"

"I'm a math major. So you probably saw me around."

He smiles. "See? I was right. I knew I saw you before. And what about you? Why did you come? Besides not having to eat caf food?"

I think about what Bijal told me a week ago. "Why not? I could live a little."

He nods. "Well, I'm glad you're here."

Caleb tells me about how he's majoring in business. His goal is to take over his family's landscaping business so his parents can retire which I think is admirable. I want to get my phD in physics so I can understand how the universe works, where we come from, and why we're here. The last two are more spiritual based than mathematical based, but the questions remain and hopefully math can help me get closer to solving it.

"Are you on the apps?" he asks me.

I tuck a braid behind my ear and think of the best way to say that I'm a horrible texter and not the best at taking pictures. "No. It just all seems...fake."

He nods. "I get what you mean. It's like people put out an image of who they want to portray and not who they actually are."

"Exactly! And you can't get to the heart of who someone is through a screen. It's just so—"

"Empty," Caleb finishes my sentence.

"Yeah. Empty." Our chests rise in unison as his stare stirs something deep within my belly. The ease and wonder this whole night has me wondering if he could be the answer to my questionable love life.

"I'm gonna leave this for y'all," the waitress interrupts our trance by sliding the bill towards Caleb.

"Don't worry. It's my treat." He reaches into his back pocket, pulls out his wallet, and slides the credit card in the check pre-senter which he hands back to the waitress. "Speaking of treat, I hope you have room for dessert. There's a Sonic down the street and it's"—he looked at his watch—"after 8."

"Half-priced shakes," we say simultaneously.

When the waitress returns, we gather our stuff and walk towards Sonic. I lean on Caleb's shoulders to help me take off my heels. Bijal was well-intentioned when she helped me get dressed tonight, but she wasn't practical. He wraps his arm around my lower waist to steady me, and a heat instantly rises from my lower back. The nervousness causes me to lose my balance and tilt.

Caleb's arm tightens around my waist. "I got you."

His lips are mere inches from mine. I look at them and back up at him before I regain my composure.

"Thanks," I sigh, hoping to release some of the tension rising in my chest.

"No problem. You okay? Cause there's the Sonic right there." He points to the marquee maybe two blocks from us.

I twist my black obsidian pendant between my fingers. "I just lost my balance. That's all."

"Okay." He bites his bottom lip. "After you."

Carrying the shoes in my hands, the concrete sidewalk indent the soles of my feet. Anything beats walking in heels. Although it's nine on a Saturday night, the street is quiet and dimly lit by a street light. When we reach Sonic, I order my favorite Oreo cheesecake shake while he gets the banana milkshake.

Sitting on top of the table, I lean back on my arms. The heaviness of summer still lingers into fall, and the humidity glues the braids to my back so I pull them away from my neck. I glance over at Caleb who's staring at me with the spoon in his mouth.

"What?"

"You're really pretty."

His gushing makes my eyes roll. He's such a try-hard.

"No. I'm serious." He puts his hand on mine, stands up, and cups my face. His thumb rubs against my jaw. I close my eyes to his cologne wafting across my nose: sandalwood and juniper. My chest heaves in anticipation. "You're fucking beautiful."

He tilts my mouth towards his and kisses me. I grab the nape of his neck so his soft lips can linger a little bit longer.

He runs his thumb across my cheek. "I had a nice time with you tonight."

His breath dances along my lips. I swallow. "Me too."

His hand travels down my neck, arm, and to my hand where he interlocks his fingers with mine. "Can I see you again? Next week? My friends and I are having a game night in the dorms."

"Yeah." My gaze travels from his lips to his bright blue eyes. "I'll be there."

"Great." He pulls his face away. "So...can I get your number or will I have to keep sliding in your DMs?"

I laugh, handing him my phone.

***

Caleb stands outside his dorm waiting for me. All he told me was that this was a casual game night with his friends and to dress comfortably. Since the fall weather is finally acting right, I'm wearing joggers and a crop top. When he reaches me, he wraps his arms around my waist, pulling me closer to him and kissing me on the forehead. "I'm so glad you came." He puts his hands on my shoulder to look me in my eyes. "Are you ready?"

"Of course. What are we playing?"

"Phase 10. You ever heard of it?"

"No."

He gasps. "You're lying?" From the look on my face, he could tell I'm not. "Well it's easy. You'll catch on quickly. There's a card that tells you what you need to do to complete your phase. A set is like four of a kind. A run is kind of like a straight." He sees the confusion I wear on my face. "Come on. Once you start playing, you'll see how easy it is."

He opens the door for me. "Just don't tell the guys you haven't played before. It's their favorite game."

I nod and follow him to a room off the side of the atrium. Once he opens that door, four guys and two girls sit at the table.

"You must be Shauna." A couple walks up to me. "I'm Tim, and this is Clarissa," the guy says, embracing me. "Sorry, I'm a hugger."

"Hi Tim and Clarissa," I manage to say despite Tim's squeezing.

"That's John and his girlfriend Lily," Caleb points to the couple on the left side of the table. "And that's Dustin and Marc." He points to the two guys on the right side of the table. All of them either wave or say hi except for Marc whose dark stare makes me shudder.

"Now that we're all here. Let's start the game," Clarissa says.

Tim shuffles the cards and passes them out. Caleb makes sure that I get an instruction card so I'll have some idea what's going on.

"So, Shauna?" Tim asks while passing out the cards. "Caleb told us you're a math major. Why would you do something like that?"

I always hated this question. The truth is that I believe that numbers hold an energy. That the more I learn about numbers, the more I understand about the world, about life, about creation. But every time I tell people that, they look at me like maybe I need a break from studying math.

"I've always been good at math. Figured I'd major in it," I settle on telling him. It seems like it's a good enough reason because the questions stop, and the game begins. I go through the first five phases rather quickly. At first, most of us complete our phases, and then it slowly dwindles and dwindles until it's just me and Marc on phase seven.

"So how did y'all meet each other? Was it here?" I ask, moving my cards around in my hand preparing to complete the phase.

Caleb stares across the table at Dustin and Tim. It's like they're waiting for the other to answer. Caleb clears his throat and answers, "We met in high school actually."

"Yeah, our parents signed us up for this...fraternity," Dustin swallows.

I can read a room. Whatever "fraternity" it is, it's not something they want to talk about.

Clarissa picks up on it too. "Shauna...you're a junior, right? Any big plans after college?"

"I'm thinking of going to State to get my PhD in physics."

"Wow. So beautiful and brilliant? Caleb, I like her." She winks at him.

Marc scoffs, and when I look at him, a fiery heat spreads across my chest. He turns away from me to face the window. Picking up on Marc's attitude, Tim redirects us back to the game. I advance to phase eight, leaving Marc at phase seven and eventually win the game by being the first to complete the ten phases.

Afterwards, I help Lily and Dustin pack up the cards. Tim gives me an equally tight goodbye hug, and Caleb offers to walk me back to my dorm. The brisk autumn air hits us once we open the door. Walking on the sidewalk, the red and yellow leaves rustle overhead, dropping a few leaves here and there. I rub my arms from the cool air.

"You cold?" Caleb asked. He wraps his arm around me and massages my outer arm. It doesn't help that much, but I appreciate the effort. "Thank you for coming tonight."

"Yeah. Your friends seem nice." I bite my lip wondering if I should say something. I hate holding things in so I decide to. "I think Marc hates me."

"Marc? Noooo," Caleb tries to defend him but shakes his head, deciding against it. "Yep. Marc's an ass. He doesn't really like anyone."

I fiddle with my protection crystal thinking that what I felt from Marc was more than dislike. White boys only stare when they want to fuck you or kill you. Sometimes both. The look in his eyes was burning hatred. Marc seems like the kind of person who believes this country is only for *real* Americans, even though my ancestors have been here as long as his.

Caleb, sensing my discomfort, rubs my back and pulls me into his chest. He rests his chin on my head. "Don't worry about Marc okay? He's an asshole."

I nod, then he slides his hand down to mine and interlocks our fingers. We're feet from my dorm when a guy in a hoodie walks past us. A scowl crosses his face when he sees our hands. He mumbles, "Fucking race traitor."

"What did you say?!" Caleb stands in the guy's face, knocking his hoodie off and causing his dreads to fly around. "What did you say to her?"

Caleb pushes him to the ground before getting on top of the guy and punching him in the face. I have only known Caleb for a few weeks, and I've never seen him so full of rage. I grab his waist to try and pull him off the guy who then gets up and runs.

"Are you okay?" he asks me, his breath heavy and shaky.

"Are *you* okay?" I grab his hand and rub my thumb over his bloody knuckles.

He holds my head, pins my braids to my ears, and presses his forehead against mine. "I'm fine," he says. Our chests heave. Our breaths, in sync. The heat of the moment still palpable between us. His lips grazes mine. "I'm fine."

Holding his hand, I unlock the door to the dorm and walk down the hallway to my room. Bijal drove home this weekend so we're all alone. Opening the door, Caleb hoists me up against the wall. His hands grasp my thighs, and his kisses line my neck with goosebumps. Blood rushes to his cheeks and mouth. Gripping my neck, he squeezes harder, smiles, and bites my bottom lip. Hunger fills his eyes. I smile back at him before pushing him towards the bed.

Our clothes fly off, and he climbs on top of me, nibbles my inner thigh, then my belly, nipple, neck, before finally landing on my lips. In one fell swoop, Caleb wraps his arm around my midsection, swings me around, and backs my thighs against his. His fingers caress my back, thighs, and butt before he plunges into me. It's slow at first, but he speeds up with a searing intensity. While thrusting, he grabs my arms, pulling them behind me with one of his hands. He uses his other arm to hold me in a chokehold. My back rears under the pressure, but he never stops thrusting.

When he finishes, he lays beside me, and I fold into his chest. Sweat glistens on our bodies. We lay in silence, waiting for our breaths to slow when he looks past me to the corner of the room. "What's that?"

Without turning around, I already know where his eyes went. It's where everyone's eyes go. The small table with white table-cloth that holds a glass of water, candle, incense, and loose tobacco. In the center of the table on a white plate are sliced apples from the cafeteria, sprinkled with cinnamon and drizzled in honey.

"It's an altar," I croak. My voice is sore, but I search for words that seem more sensible and less woo-woo. "You know how churches have altars? Anybody can have one."

"Why?"

"To remember the dead."

"Oh." He turns on his back and looks up at the ceiling. "I guess once people are in the ground, I just never think of them anymore."

"Most people don't."

***

I zip my duffle bag and sit it on my bed next to my sleeping bag.

"Are you sure you still want to go camping tonight? It's gonna get like fifty-five degrees." Concern grows on Bijal's face.

"I'll be fine, Bijal. You worry too much," I try to reassure her. Honestly, I'm the worried one. The idea of spending the night under the stars with Caleb is romantic, but it's a group trip which means Marc will be there. I haven't seen him since the Phase 10 game over a month ago. I could barely stomach a few hours with him. How will I hold up a whole night?

"You were the one who told me to live a little," I remind her. "I'm living. Plus I can snuggle under Caleb all night."

"I still can't believe that you're dating Caleb Willard." She stands in front of me and holds my hands. "I want you to have fun, but I want you to be safe. Call me if anything happens."

"You know I will."

She hugs me before sending me out the door. Caleb's waiting outside in his pickup truck. He flashes a smile when he sees me which makes my stomach flutter.

"You excited?" he asks when I open the door.

"Yeah." I push my worries down with a smile and place my bag in the back seat. Besides the music on the radio, we mostly drive in silence. He turns onto I-55, switches to I-20 and then turns onto Highway 43 going towards Pelahatchie. The roads get smaller and rougher as asphalt turns to gravel. Once in Pela-hatchie, the stars twinkle in the moonless sky, and the sounds of the cicadas grow. Uncertainty swells in my stomach, but I swallow it down. We turn, and there's a car in the middle of the road, blocking the path ahead.

"What the fuck?" Caleb says. He flicks between his bright and low beams to try and signal the car. "I'll check it out."

"Don't." I grab his arm. "I don't have a good feeling about this."

He touches my hand. "Don't worry." He reaches in the back and grabs his shotgun. "I'll be back."

I lock the truck, bite my lip, and twist my pendant between my fingers. He slowly approaches the car with his shotgun upright and leading the way. He peeps into the driver's side, but no one's there. There's no one in the backseat either. He shrugs and walks back to the truck. I unlock the doors but feel when someone else opens my door behind me. Something heavy hits my head.

The cold wakes me up. Dirt fills my mouth. I try to move but can't. My hands are tied behind me, and something heavy lays on my neck. My head's covered, and all I can see are two round lights that look like headbeams.

"The bitch is up!"

That voice. It sounds familiar.

The heavy thing wraps around my neck pulling me up to my knees. I choke. The bag covering my head is yanked off. My vision is blurry, but I can make out the face shining in the light of the head beams: Marc.

He squeezes my chin and lets out a crooked smile. "I been waiting to snuff out that ball of sunshine since the first time I saw you."

My lips curl in disgust. He pushes my face away and spits on me. I look down to see what's around my neck—a rope—and over to where the rope is—in Dustin's hands. I shake my head. A tear falls and betrays me. As much as I don't want it to be true, I know.

"Oh the nigger gets it now. You looking for lover boy?"

He turns my face to the side of the truck, and there he is. His arms are crossed, jaw clenched, and the blues of his eyes darkened.

"If it makes you feel better,"—Marc's mouth is against my ear—"he said you were one of his favorites."

He shoves my face away. "String her up!"

The rope slowly tightens around my neck pulling me up from the ground. My chest heaves under the weight of the truth. Tears fall from my face, but I'm determined not to be an offering for their gods. I mouth their names, "Catherine Mae, Lealer, Blanche, Rachel, Lucy, Matilda."

Marc, seeing my mouth move, says "Oh, your god can't help you now!"

Afraid of their true power, I refused to address them all—calling only on the benevolent ones. But desperate times call for "And every ancestor I don't know. And every spirit whose blood is soaked in this ground."

My plea is simple: "Help."

The rope wraps around my neck dangling my feet in the air. My back rears from the pressure. I wiggle trying to free myself when Dustin starts coughing. He reaches for his neck trying to pry off something that isn't there. The rope loosens, dropping me to the ground. My neck burns. A chorus of knees joins me. They cough. Blood pours from their crevices, and long tinges of red drool fall from their mouth. Each reaches for an invisible noose around their neck. Some plead for their lives. Others turn blue. A dozen of them fall. Marc seems to get the worst of this, fighting his own body to expend the last drop of energy cursing me. Only one is left standing.

"What did you do to them?" Caleb asks.

"What I'm about to do to you." The blood-stained voice that leaves my body doesn't sound like my own.

He looks behind me in horror. I turn around to see them: the forgotten. Their eyes— black as obsidian—never lift from Caleb's body. As they circle him, he struggles to breathe. The ghosts of a thousand hands squeeze his neck. Blood streams from his eyes lining his cheek, but his gaze never leaves mine. My heart thuds. The fear that filled me now fills him, and I watch as the army of ancestors take his last breath.

The Pastor's Wife

A week before Chanel's wedding, I dreamt that her husband would be the death of her. In the dream, he chased her down a dark alley, eventually cornering her, leaving her with nowhere to go. When he put his hands on her, everything went black, and I woke up.

I didn't think it'd come true.

It had been many years since I'd seen Chanel, and many more after that dream when I'd see her again. I saw the wedding announcement in the newspaper. Her joy was visible even from that still image.

My clairvoyance was new then, and I was untrustworthy; I didn't want it to be true, but here Chanel laid, twenty-eight, dead in a white casket. The after-death bloat brought back a bit of vitality to her body. Her face was soft now instead of gaunt. As people filed into the church, my heart tightened watching her lay there. She was finally at peace, but we weren't.

She was my cousin, only a few months younger than me. We went to daycare, elementary, and high school together. At family reunions, we would run off and gossip about school and boys. A decade ago, when we were teenagers on our way to college, we sat in her car after the morning service. Her golden face gleamed with possibility as she told me about her college plans. She was going to State with Brian, and after college, they'd get married and start a family. It was the blueprint for all girls our age so I wasn't surprised when she asked me if I'd marry Darrell, my high school sweetheart, after college. I wasn't sure, but I was excited to leave the state in search of something more promising, something more ancient. I promised her that once I left, I'd never step foot in this church again.

I lied.

After the choir sang and the prayer was prayed, her husband eulogized her. He stood behind the pulpit with his head bowed, thinking, searching for the right way to lie.

"We're gathered here today to celebrate the life of my beautiful wife, Chanel Leroy." His hands on the top of the podium, he shifted trying to force or hold back tears. "You know, Proverbs 18:22 says, *Whoso findeth a wife findeth a good thing, and obtaineth favour of the Lord.* I was a lucky man," he said, nodding with red eyes. "Chanel was every good thing God could give me: loyal, honest, submissive. Her faith in me made me a better man." He twisted his mouth.

I shifted in my seat and started fanning myself. The pew directly in front of Pastor Leroy, which should have been filled with Chanel's family and closest friends was instead filled with some congregants wearing their good brassieres. When the Pastor's eyes would drift their way, they'd lift the scarfs from over their skirts. He'd bow his head again and blot the sweat from his forehead.

"I heard she got cancer," a woman sitting in the pew in front of me whispered behind her fan to the lady next to her.

"She probably got a hold of that *stuff*," the lady whispered back to her.

"Mmmm, Lord have mercy," the woman replied, fanning herself. "How long you think before the Pastor has a new wife?"

"You know how he is." They stifled their giggles behind their fans.

I sighed. My dear Chanel, was it worth it?

When Pastor Leroy finished his eulogy, Aunt Marie gave her remarks. A few girls from high school gave theirs. They cried about how they hadn't seen Chanel in so long, how much they missed her, and how she was gone too soon. I sat there. I had no words to describe how my own insecurities failed her. How if I had trusted myself, maybe she wouldn't have been in this position. A tear fell from my eye, so I paid it my respect by letting it linger instead of rushing to wipe it away.

The deacon stood next to the altar to read the closing scripture. "Can everyone turn their Bibles to Ecclesiastes chapter three?"

It was Chanel's favorite verse.

Pages flipped in the church before the deacon cleared his throat and spoke, "Ecclesiastes chapter three, verses one through eight reads as follows: *To every thing there is a season, and a time to every purpose under the heaven: A time to be born, and a time to die; a time to plant, and a time to pluck up that which is planted; A time to kill, and a time to heal; a time to break down, and a time to build up; A time to weep, and a time to laugh; a time to mourn, and a time to dance; A time to cast away stones, and a time to gather stones together; a time to embrace, and a time to refrain from embracing; A time to get, and a time to lose; a time to keep, and a time to cast away; A time to rend, and a time to sew; a time to keep silence, and a time to speak; A time to love, and a time to hate; a time of war, and a time of peace.* That is the word of God for the people of God."

And the congregation said, "Amen."

"Now, may we all stand and sing Amazing Grace before we lay Chanel in her final resting place," Pastor Leroy commanded.

We stood. He started the song with his shaky baritone, rocking behind the pulpit until his eyes met mine. He gulped and averted his gaze, but mine never left his face. After he prayed the benediction, half the church readied themselves for the procession. I stayed for one last look at Chanel. I followed the giggling behind me and saw that Pastor Leroy stepped out from behind the pulpit. One of the women from the front pew rubbed his arm while another offered to cook him dinner. Once he saw the eyes on him, he shooed them away and walked towards me.

"Sister Simone, I'm surprised to see you here," he said.

"I don't see why not. Chanel's my baby cousin."

"Well you're always welcome back here. It's never too late to get right with God."

I stared at him. My jaw clenched. "It's not *my* soul you need to worry about, Pastor."

"Well," he backed up. "I guess I'll be seeing you at the burial."

"I guess so," I sucked my teeth and caressed Chanel's cold, puffy face.

It had been a month since I last saw her alive. She rushed into my house on a Tuesday afternoon. The love spell I gave her was wearing off; she needed something stronger.

"He has a child on the way," she cried while pacing in front of my couch. "I...I don't know what else to do."

"Can you sit down?" I tried to calm her. "Are you hungry? Can I get you anything?"

The stress ate the meat off her bones. Her clavicle protruded from the blouse that enveloped her. The skirt she wore threatened to fall off at any second. The tangled wig sat sideways on her head.

"I'm not hungry," she said, still pacing and biting her nails.

"Can you sit, please? All your pacing is making me dizzy."

She sat beside me, but now her leg bounced. It'd do for now.

"Simone." She held my hands. "Is there anything you can do to make this baby go away?"

"I can't," I told her. I couldn't imagine doing such a thing. "Did you ask your husband about it?"

She looked betrayed that I even asked her. "He lies about everything. Everytime I confront him, he says it's the devil driving us apart." Her lip quivered in frustration. "I don't know how much more of this I can take."

"You can leave," I offered.

"And go where?" She was up again, pacing. "I can't just leave my husband, the church. I have an image to uphold. You wouldn't understand."

"And why wouldn't I?"

She shook her head and sat next to me. "You've always been brave, Simone. I haven't. I wish I could do half the things you do."

"I'm not brave," I confessed. "I have fears and insecurities too."

"Not like me."

I sighed and shifted my body towards her, holding her hands. "I didn't leave Darrell because I didn't love him. You know how they raise boys here. I left because I was afraid of losing my freedom if I married him. I was afraid that I wouldn't survive that kind of life." *I was afraid that I'd end up like you* was what I didn't tell her.

She sighed, tucking her head in her hands, "You know, Mother Denuit told me that this is just how men are. That real women stick by their men, and if I was a real woman, I wouldn't make a scene." The tears fell from her eyes into her trembling hands.

I rubbed her back. Mother Denuit would know. Deacon Denuit was the father to my cousin Letitia and a host of other kids that were not Mother Denuit's. "You can choose differently."

She clasped her hands and shook her head. Through tears she confessed, "I can't."

Looking at her cry, she was a shell of her former self. In high school, Chanel was the It Girl. Everyone wanted to be like her, dress like her, act like her. Boys groveled at her feet. It was I who was envious of her, the way she walked through the world with the power to make life happen, but the power she had was given, not innate. She had all the choices in the world, but like most girls in our small town, she wanted to be a wife and a mother.

By thirteen, she had planned her ring, dress, and season. At twenty, after Brian dumped her, she only entertained potential husbands. And at twenty-two, when half the girls from high school were married, she was single and desperate. Within the year, she married Pierre Leroy. Five years later, she sat on my couch crying over him.

"You know," she sniffed; the tears sobered her up a bit. "When we were younger, I could imagine a future with every boy I ever dated. But Pierre? Pierre was different. When I'd see our future, I just saw black. I thought it meant that it was still forming, that the possibilities were endless, but now?" She sighed again. "I don't know what to think."

She was right. When we dreamed of our future, we dreamt of possibility, but the blackness itself was a possibility, albeit an absolute one.

"Can you help me?" Her red eyes sunk into her bony face.

My chest tightened knowing that the strongest spells had the highest cost: blood.

"I can."

"Will he love me?"

I wanted to tell her that a man that didn't respect her could never love her, but she had dedicated her life to him so instead I offered her hope. "He will," I said.

And she took comfort in the lie.

The Dentverine

A iden Michaels is a Dentverine I sensed weeks ago. Eating my lunch outside, I watch him laughing boisterously, head cocked back with his hands on his chest. Echoes of his laughter reach me at the edge of the food court. He's surrounded by a posse of friends who probably only know him as the school's quarterback, the Captain's son, and the golden boy.

When I finish lunch, I head to my locker to get my books for my next class. I hear a "Hey you!" and shut the locker door to see Aiden waving. I look behind me for his intended recipient before realizing it's me.

He's sensed me.

"You're the new girl, right?" Aiden asks, strolling up to my locker. He smiles showing perfect pointy canines. His blue-green eyes mimic mine as well as his olive skin and shiny black curly hair.

"I've been here for a month. Not exactly new," I reply.

He flashes his canines. "Walk with me."

It's a command. He's so used to getting his way that he starts walking expecting me to follow. I do.

It's a gray day, the thick clouds blanket the sky as we walk outside, far away from my next class, but that doesn't matter. I'm finally alone with Aiden Michaels.

"I'm Aiden, by the way," he says, with his hand to his chest, forcing an introduction.

"Saraya," I play along.

"Pretty name."

He gives me the once-over, and I suppress the need to roll my eyes. He's flirting.

"Do you ever see someone, and it triggers feelings so deep in you that you have to say something?"

I snicker. This one has a way with words.

"It's a blood attraction, not a romantic one," I explain.

His eyebrows knit together, and he shakes his head. I stop walking so I can face him. How much does he know about this? Let's cut to the chase and find out.

"You're a Dentverine."

His head jerks, looking over his shoulder before he grabs my arm and whispers aggressively, "I have no idea what you're talking about."

"You just admitted to sensing me."

"You're a Dentverine?" he whispers as his eyes widen. Now he's getting it. "But how are you normal?"

"I'm not normal."

"But you're not—" He curls his fingers into claws and snarls.

"I'm not a full Dentverine and I haven't turned. I'm part, like you."

"But you've controlled it?"

"You can't control your Dentverine side. You can only accept it."

He scratches his chin as he considers this. It seems like whichever parent is Dentverine never told him the basics.

"So there are full Dents, turned Dents, and there are us," I explain. "Full Dents have no human in them. They get a bad rap of being ferocious beasts, but they're surprisingly mild when you get to know them."

"You know full Dentverines?" His voice is a mixture of awe and fear.

"Yes, they taught me how to accept my Dentverine side."

"But how do you, you know, talk to a Dentverine?"

"We sense each other. We can sense thoughts, feelings, memories, everything."

"Oh. So, how do the turned Dentverines work? I thought once you turned Dent, you don't turn back?" he asks.

"It depends on how you turn," I explain. "If you've accepted your Dent side, you can shift between the two, but many part Dents are so full of bitterness and resentment for the cards they've been dealt that they take it out on humans and Dents, alike. When you succumb to the bitterness, you become a danger to everyone, including yourself."

"And if I can't get it under control, I'll be a turned Dentver-ine?"

"If you don't accept it, yes."

He nods along. "So, can you help me figure out this whole thing?"

"I can."

"Cool." He scratches his neck. "Are you busy this weekend? My dad's throwing a party, and I can introduce you to my friends. It's just if they see us together, they're gonna ask questions, and I can't exactly say I'm part Dentverine, you know, and if—"

"I'll be there," I chuckle, cutting off his anxious rambling.

***

As I turn down a driveway with densely packed trees over-head, a white two-story house comes into view. Every room has floor-to-ceiling windows, and dance music blasts from speakers while people walk around with wine glasses or red solo cups in hand. I crack my knuckles walking towards the house, a bit nervous to introduce myself. Thankfully Aiden meets me at the door, his canines flashing in his signature smile. When he hugs me, he smells like a mix of pine and compost.

"Thanks for coming. Remind me to snatch you away for a lesson." He wags his finger in my face, and I chuckle.

He leads me to the kitchen island where his posse is posed. There's Noah and Ethan, Aiden's teammates and best friends. Kai, the slim blue-haired enby. Malia, Aiden's Barbie-doll not girlfriend girlfriend, and Chloe, Malia's best friend.

I stand beside Aiden as he introduces me, ingesting the stares and silent judgments of his friends. Before he walks away, he pats me on the shoulder and whispers near my ear. "They won't hurt you. They just look like they will."

Kai rises from the chair they're sitting in. "You just moved here, right?"

"Yeah, from the Coast."

Eyebrows raise.

"Why would you move here?" Chloe asks.

"I'd take the Coast any day," Kai comments.

"Moved in with my aunt," I say.

"What about your parents?" Kai asks.

"They're dead."

Everyone's silent as usual, faces turned downward in pity for the orphan girl. I've been through this before. I brave a smile to show how over it I am. My parents are dead. I'm fine. Let's move on.

"I'm so sorry," Chloe says.

I clear my throat to stop it from closing. "It's okay."

"If you ever want to talk, we're here." Kai rubs my shoulder.

I offer them a small smile and hope that that will change the subject, but thankfully Malia does.

"So how did you and Aiden meet?"

Chloe slaps her arm and mumbles something to her.

"We're working on a project together," I reply.

"For?"

"History."

She drops it from there. The last thing I want is to date Aiden. Kai grabs my hand and leads me away from the group and their questions. At the counter, they ask twice if I want any alcohol in my drink. "The Captain's cool. He doesn't care at all."

"I'm good," I reassure them. When they leave me alone, I take a seat in the corner of the room and sip my soda. I watch everyone in their small groups, chatting enthusiastically about nothing that really matters. Glancing out the window, I search for Aiden but can't find him.

"Just gonna squeeze in here if you don't mind." An older pale man motions behind me to a liquor cabinet.

"Sorry," I say and shuffle out of his way.

'You're one of my son's friends?" he asks. It's Captain Michaels.

"Aiden? Yeah. I'm Saraya."

"Pretty name."

Like father, like son. With ice and brown liquor in his glass, he leans against the bar, crossing his legs. He takes a slow sip from the glass then holds the drink in front of him. I fill the silence with a sip of lemon-lime soda. I don't get the usual full-body sensations when I'm near a Dentverine. No emotions or thoughts. Captain Michaels is fully human.

"I haven't seen you around much," he says.

"Yep. Just moved here."

"And you're already friends with my son?" he asks.

"We have a lot in common." I wonder how much Mayor Michaels knows about the part Aiden and I share.

He sips his drink then nods. He gives me the once over before saying, "I like you. I think you'd be good for him. Much better than—" He waves his drink in the direction of Malia.

I stare at her with her big brown eyes, button nose, and full lips that lend to her beauty. One look at her rich brown skin, though, helps me realize why Mayor Michaels doesn't think she's good enough for Aiden, and why he thinks I'd be better.

"Respectfully, sir, I'm not interested in Aiden in that way."

"So you're a queer? It's fine if you are," he rushes to add.

I fake a smile. "It was nice meeting you."

I hustle out the door and lean against the wall, exhaling deeply. I can see why Aiden wants to be "normal" and get rid of his Dentverine side. It can't be easy when his dad doesn't like too much "difference" in his son's life.

"You ready for that lesson?" Aiden asks, grinning. He snuck up on me.

"Yeah." I nod, desperate to distance myself from the mess inside.

"Let's walk."

The earthy notes hanging in the air relax me. Once we're some distance from the party, I tell him, "So...I met your father."

He winces. "Sorry about that. I should've warned you."

"He hates Malia?" I ask.

"Yeah. He doesn't think I should date her."

"But you like Malia?"

He smashes his lips together in a sad smile.

"It's your life, Aiden. Date who you want."

He grunts like life isn't as simple as accepting who you are and dating who you want.

"I, um—" He scratches his neck. It must be a nervous tic. "I heard about your parents. I'm sorry. My mom died giving birth to me."

"I'm sorry about your mom." He must've inherited his Dent side from her.

"I never knew her," he shrugs, looking down at his feet as we walk.

"My dad was a Dent." I pause before adding the rest. "He killed my mom."

"Oh shit."

I nod, swallowing the grief that wants to swell in my throat. "My dad was trying to control his Dent side. He fought his whole life and lost."

I remember how hard he tried to be normal for me and Mom. How much he altered his natural way of being, hoping that if he fought harder, one day he'd be fully human. But you can't change yourself into something that you're not. Now knowing that your Dent and human side can peacefully coexist, I'm upset Dad didn't learn how to accept himself sooner. Doing so would've saved our family.

"What happened to your Dad? Afterwards?"

My jaw clenches, and I swallow. Before I answer, I inhale and then say, "I put him down."

"Saraya." Aiden's breath hitches.

"It was a mercy killing," I explain. "Dad had turned. He was bound to lash out at me and other innocent creatures with his personal suffering. It had to be done."

When I turn to Aiden, his hands are shoved into his pockets, his jaw and neck tense. I hope he realizes how important this is. Acceptance is life or death. To help him understand I offer him the truth.

"There was a pack of turned Dents headed in this direction a few weeks ago. When I sensed you, I realized that they may be headed here to try and turn you, get you to join their pack."

His identity crisis sent a distress signal our way. I'm just glad I got to him before the others did.

He shakes his head. "You can't just walk into my life and tell me all this. It's a lot, Saraya."

"I know, but I'm trying to help you. That's why it's important you accept your Dent side before they get to you."

"But I never asked for any of this. I just want to be normal."

"It's okay to not be normal."

"Being a monster is not okay."

"Do you think I'm a monster?"

I stare at him, wanting him to say it to my face. Is being part Dent really the worst thing in the world? Instead of facing me, he looks out toward the woods. Coward.

"You know what I mean. I can't pull off the mysterious loner like you."

I'm not sure if that's a compliment or an insult, but I leave it alone. He waves his hand back towards the house. "Everybody in there likes me for who I pretend to be. If they know I'm part, you know, they'll leave."

There's a sadness in his voice. I see how badly he needs the connection, the love, but it's only conditional on his being human. He's not that.

"You don't know if they'll accept you or not," I say. "You haven't given them a chance to know you as part Dent."

"I know my dad hates Dentverines."

Who doesn't his dad hate? Aiden's frustration carries over to me. I can't imagine the loneliness of finding out you're a Dentverine and having no one to talk to about it, knowing the only parent you have will hate you for it. The leaves rustle behind us and simultaneously, Aiden and I feel it: a Dent.

"Go back to the house," I tell him, relaxing into the transformation.

"Are you sure?" He plants his feet on the ground, preparing to fight.

"You shouldn't be here. I got it."

When we're in the presence of a turned or full Dent, our bodies transform involuntarily. We can either accept that transformation or resist it. Aiden's not ready for either yet.

As he runs away, I shift into my teeth sharpening and lengthening, my fingers turning into claws, and my body becoming stronger and hairier. I slink toward the place where we heard the leaves rustling and a Dent is on all fours. Fear and confusion overwhelm me, and I realize that she's scared. Her memories show that she's just turned. She's fourteen and needs guidance. I share that I'm here to help, and she listens, following me to a safe place away from the party.

***

During Biology class, the lights go out. We're not under any severe weather notices, but the emergency system comes on informing us to go to the auditorium. I meet up with Aiden in the hallway.

"Does this kind of thing normally happen?" I ask while students shuffle around us.

"No, it—" He stops. Furious rage swells in my chest. They're here.

"You feel that?" I ask Aiden.

"Feel what?" Malia asks from behind me.

My heartbeat quickens.

"Son, you're okay." Captain Michaels hugs Aiden.

"Dad, what are you doing here?"

"Dentverines are here."

Aiden and I glance at each other. They're here for him. I've only had a week with Aiden. That's barely enough time to help him understand what a Dent is, never mind embrace being one. He still believes he can stop himself from turning and spiraling into despair. He's ripe prey for the turned Dents.

"Go to the auditorium," Captain Michaels instructs. "We'll try and lure them away."

"Stay close to me," I whisper to Aiden.

Malia latches onto his other side. When we get into the auditorium, Aiden files in with Malia and me behind him. We watch the students fill in the rows as chatter speculating what's happening rises. Principal Conners taps the mic to settle everyone.

"Students, please find a seat. Now we don't want you to worry. This is just a safety—"

A Dent swoops from the trusses above and grabs Principal Conners by the head, effectively decapitating him. His blood splatters on the stage and the front row. A metallic taste coats my tongue while the screams of people running toward the exits fill the auditorium. I look over at Aiden whose teeth are lengthening and crowding his mouth. Reaching behind Malia, I sink my claws into his arm, hoping that it'll be enough to distract him from turning. My heart is a cacophony, and I try to count the layers of beats there. Six. I count six heartbeats. Mine, Aiden's, and four Dents.

Aiden buries his head in his lap, and Malia tries to calm him. My nails sharpen into knives.

"Malia, you should get everyone out of here."

"Something's wrong with Aiden." She turns around to face me, and her eyes widen. Fear. It's part of the trinity that you have to accept about being a Dent—the fear, anger, and hatred that humans will have for you simply existing as something different.

"What are you?" she asks, the horror growing on her face.

"Malia, go!" I growl.

Aiden lifts his transforming head. Stalactites of teeth overtake his face which is covered in hair. He's fighting, digging his claws into his chest to avoid attacking Malia.

"Aiden?" she asks, leaning in to get a closer look.

"Go!" I push Malia out of the way, right before Aiden launches at her.

His anger, hurt, and resentment are pulsing through my veins. He didn't want Malia to see him like that. He doesn't want any of this to be happening. I can feel that, and I can feel the Dents closing in on us.

"Aiden, you have to quit fighting."

"No," he grunts. His claws rip his shirt off, and his self-inflicted wounds are healing.

"Aiden, the more you fight, the worse it'll be."

His blue-green eyes now flash red. His pulse quickens as his head leans to the side, considering me. He's giving in to the bitterness. He's turning. I shrug into my Dent form.

Aiden, please. I don't want to hurt you, I share.

My paw's extended to keep him at bay. His body slowly turns, muscles forming and tightening, claws growing. Hair rushes to cover the lower half of his body.

Aiden, please.

He doesn't respond to me. The rage filling his mind now fills mine. He paces before launching his body through the air. I slide to dodge his attack. A snarl reaches my ear. Over my shoulder, another Dent drops from the trusses but waits. She's...curious? Does she want me, too?

Before I can think about it, Aiden rushes me and slices into my side. I howl.

Aiden, you don't have to do this.

I press my wound, but Aiden is still unresponsive. He tries to gouge my other side, but my paw stops him. Back and forth he strikes me, and I stop his blows until he pins me on the floor, stretches his claws, and reaches for my chest. I struggle, pushing his paw away from me. With all my strength, I push. My claw gashes into his chest, a kill strike. He yelps. His body droops around my claw. When I retract it, he falls to the floor, and I relax into my human form.

"I'm sorry, friend," I say, cradling his head in my lap.

Thank you, he shares. He'd rather be dead than a "monster."

I bring his head to my chest to hold him. The salt of my tears mixes with the blood of his wound. I'll go after the other Dents next, but for now, I hold my friend, his heart rattling in his chest until his last breath.

Collapsed

The air is stale with the stench of rats dead and alive. They squeak as I step over the piles of garbage, left from previous scavengers. Although the hairs on my arms stand, I breathe through it, shuffling through the trash on the floor and walking further into the kitchen. Light pours in from the hole in the roof as I open a cabinet to rats eating another one. I jump but quickly reorient to scan the shelves: wrappers, empty bottles, rat chewed package of rice. If it wasn't for the droppings in them, I'd try to salvage the rice. In the back corner, there's a can of tuna. The label is chewed off except for the logo. I snatch it before the rats attack me and inspect the can. No puncture marks. It should be good enough for Chi.

Opening the next cabinet, the rats dance in the powders of expired cake mix, flour, and sugar. I shiver then quickly scan for anything usable and find a glass jar of thick black liquid. If it wasn't for the dipper logo, I wouldn't have known it was honey. As I shove that in my bag with the tuna, tires crunch on the gravel driveway. I freeze as doors open and shut.

"I'll check around back, and you check the house for scavengers," a man says.

I tip toe and hide behind the bar separating the kitchen from the living room, but the trash whistles with each step. Someone walks up to the door and flashes a light down the corridor.

"Hello?" a woman asks.

I say nothing, squeezing my mouth and eyes shut as the rats climb over and around me. The light flashes over my head while I crouch behind the bar. She yells, "Jesus!"

"What is it?" the man calls.

"This place is covered in rats."

"Is anyone in there?" The man's voice is closer now. "We have to confirm that there are no scavengers."

He leaves and then she makes a sound as if she's shuddering. Her footsteps close in on me, and with each step, my heart rings louder in my ears. When she's beside me, I crawl behind her, jump on her back, cover her mouth, then snap her neck. She goes quietly, and I gently lay her body on the ground. I search her and find a gun. Now for the man.

I creep to the open door, peek out, and scan the coast. It's clear. I scurry to another corner of the house, searching for him. When I don't see him, I go to the next corner and catch his head peeking out from behind the shed. I raise the gun, level the nozzle with his jaw, and shoot. The birds rush out of the trees from the sound as he slinks to the ground. With the gun between us, I edge closer to him, kicking his body to make sure he's dead. Squatting, I search him and find another gun and a badge: FISCO. This country loves hiding hate behind acronyms so who knows what it means? I doubt it's good.

I look for money, food, or keys but find nothing. Returning to the house, I search the woman. Although she looks a tad bit bigger than me, her clothes would probably fit. I strip her of the badge, black t-shirt, tactical pants, belt, and shoes and leave her body there for the rats.

Walking down the decaying road, I stay close to the tree line, in case more FISCO agents come. Around dusk, I return to the old apartment complex Chi and I have been squatting in. I knock—three short, one long, then three more short knocks so he knows it's me. When I open the door, he runs to me.

"Gada, I didn't think you made it."

Although he's only fifteen years old, he's already taller than me. His deep voice may signal he's a man, but he's still my baby brother.

"I'm fine, Chi." I reach into my bag and pull out the can of tuna. "This is for you."

His hungry eyes look at the can in his hand and back to me. I watch as he splits the can in half with his bare hands. He scoops his finger into each half and stuffs the tuna in his mouth. My bittersweet smile remembers that it was only three years ago when his super strength activated, but what good is strength when the world is ending?

Around that time, the revolution started. The United States, a country founded on division, fought over those divisions many times since its inception, but we learned too much of what was previously hidden from us. The government never had our best interest at heart. They knew how to curtail the zombie virus but let it run rampant and destroy millions of lives. All for profit. The rich—after robbing us blind of resources, a habitable planet, and life itself—hopped on a spacecraft to destroy another planet. Then it felt like the universe threw us a hail mary when they gave Black people superpowers, but that backfired into a war on Black children.

Everyone was divided. Government versus citizens. Rich versus poor. Human versus superhuman. Adult versus children. Everyone was angry. Everyone was hurt.

No one won.

I pop the lid of the honey jar and scoop some out with my fingers to eat it. It's acrid, but I swallow it anyway. Chi finishes scarfing down his tuna, and we lay there as the sun sets, casting the apartment in darkness.

When I wake, Chi examines the badge in his hand. I snatch it from him.

"Where did you get that?" he asks.

"It doesn't matter."

"What's FISCO?"

"Who knows?"

"What are you going to do with it?"

I groan, rubbing my eyes. "Chi, it's too early for this."

"I've been thinking." He sits against the wall. "There's no picture on the badge, and you have the clothes—"

I glare at him for invading my privacy and snatch my sack from off the floor. He continues with his thoughts.

"What if you impersonate this person? Find out what FISCO is. If they have guns, they probably have food."

"It's too dangerous."

"So is staying here."

"We'll get by."

"Gada." He rises off the floor and reaches me in two paces. "This may be our only real chance of surviving. We have to take it."

"No," I insist. "What if something happens to me? I have to take care of you."

"I'm a man." He deepens his voice then grins.

I roll my eyes. "You're fifteen."

His smile sobers when he says, "Please, Gada. We have to try."

"This is a stupid idea." So is walking for miles and fighting rats for food. I exhale realizing he may be right even if it's risky. "Fine. I'll do it."

He pumps his fist in the air, and I change into the clothes, tucking the t-shirt into the pants like the woman had. I have to tighten the belt a bit more because of the bagginess of the pants. Then I pin the badge onto the collar of my shirt and tuck the gun in my waistband. When I show Chi, he gasps.

"You look like a soldier."

I wish we had a mirror so I can see myself, but I'll just have to take his word for it. We decide that I'll walk back towards the house, near the car. Maybe FISCO discovered that their agents were missing and went looking for them. Then they'll pick me up. We created a cover story, hoping that it'll give me some credibility. Before I left the apartment, I gave a gun to Chi to use just in case. Hopefully I'll be back before then.

As I'm walking down the dilapidated old highway, wheels slow down behind me. I turn to wave it down. My heart pounds against my chest, but I maintain a neutral face. When the tank slows, a window rolls down, and a gun is aimed at me. I raise my hands, and a man's eyes gaze at my body, stopping at my badge.

"Get in." He nods towards the back.

My stomach leadens, but I do. The back door opens to other soldiers sitting on either side of the van. I slide in near the door and tuck my hands between my thighs. When I look up to the row across from me, a guy's nose scrunches in disgust. The woman next to me tries her best not to breathe. It's then that I realize that although I look like them, I don't smell like them. The door shuts, and we're cast into darkness. No one talks, and I'm grateful.

The tank speeds down bumpy roads, and we're tossed around like rag dolls for what feels like an hour. I try to squeeze my body together to contain my smell and not out myself. The tank slows and eventually stops. The door opens to a spacious hangar, and a man wearing all black holds the door for us. I let everyone go in front of me so I can blend in and follow. After I step out of the tanks, the man yells to "fucking shower" and waves in front of his nose.

I shrink into the group, following them to the elevators. Although I probably should take an elevator alone, I don't know where I'm going. When I walk into it, a person presses buttons for people. They ask me, "What floor?" and I stutter.

"Check your badge," they say.

I do, and it's just a bunch of numbers: 6794313

"First number is your floor number. It took me a while to get used to this place as well." They share a small smile.

"Six," I tell them, and they press the button.

When the door to the sixth floor opens up, they remind me, "Your room number is the last two numbers."

"Thank you," I say as the door closes.

Room 13. I walk down the tiled hallway when I realize that whatever this place is has electricity. The fluorescent lights are brighter than I'm used to, but I follow the odd numbers on the left side of the hallway until I reach room thirteen. I press the badge against the scanner, and the door unlocks. It opens to a room so small that only a twin bed with a tiny nightstand fits. On the left are two doors: one to a closet and the other to the bathroom. I walk to the bathroom and see a toilet, sink, and shower.

Stripping out of the clothes, I turn the knob to the hottest setting and slip in. The water rhythmically pelts against my body, and I just stand there, eyes closed, savoring this little bit of luxury. When I open them, rivers of dirt flow down my body. Three dispensers are mounted on the wall. I press the clear one, rub it in my hand, then smell it. It smells like an artificial clean. I rub it through my hair, scrub my patchy scalp, and moan as it lathers. Then I rinse it out. The hot water trickles through my scalp and down my back. I shampoo again and then pick the cream colored liquid. When it lathers, I use it to scrub the layers of grime off my skin. I repeat, watching the water slowly turn from black to brown to clear. Squeezing the last dispenser, I distribute the conditioner through my patchy hair, letting it soften. By the time I rinse it out, the water has cooled to a lukewarm stream.

Stepping out of the shower, I grab the towel hanging by the door and use it to scrub my skin dry, then I rub it against my head. There's a bottle of lotion on the sink that I massage into my skin. When I finish all of that, I'm so overcome with exhaustion that I lay in the bed and don't even remember going to sleep.

The alarm wakes me. It's 5:30. Slowly, I pull the covers off of me and sit on the edge of the bed. The smell of something greasy floats towards my nose, and my stomach growls in response. Outside my door lies a tray with a bottle of juice and a dish with bacon, eggs, toast, and an apple. I look down the hallway and see others pulling their tray into their rooms so I do the same. Sitting on the bed, I shovel the eggs and bacon in my mouth, barely registering the crispy saltiness of the bacon or the thick goo of the eggs. I swallow the toast in two bites and wash it down with the juice. I decide to save the apple for Chi when I see him again. We agreed to wait three days before he worries about my well-being. Until then, I'm going to try and get as much food as I can before I go back to him.

When I finish my food, I set the tray back outside and go to the bathroom. Looking in the mirror, I take stock of my patchy hair. Staying clean was bad enough without running water so Chi and I often took scissors to our hair and cut it out to avoid dealing with it. I search in the cabinet under the sink for any cutting tools and find a pair of clippers. I flip the button and jump from the vibration in my hands. Leaning into the mirror, I cut the patches of hair off until my head is as smooth and even as I can make it. When I finish, I check the closet for clothes and find two more pairs of tactical pants and T-shirts, and two sets of white blouses and dress pants. I grab the tactical pants and T-shirt. As I'm dressing there's a knock on the door, and I freeze. Hopefully, whoever it is is mistaken, and they'll leave.

They knock again so I answer the door.

"We're working the floor today." He checks out my outfit. "Why are you wearing field gear?"

I look down at my clothes and then back up at him. He exhales through his nose and tries again.

"You're 4313, right? We're scheduled to work the floor together. Change clothes."

4313? The badge number. Right. I close the door and switch into the blouse and dress pants. I even find a pair of dress shoes in the bottom of the closet. When I put them on, they pinch my toes, but I have to suffer through it to blend in. I open the door to him still standing there with that impatient look on his face. When I follow him, I notice the tray is already gone.

We enter the elevator, and he presses the star button. As the elevator moves, my mind races. Has he worked with 4313 before? Does he know I'm not her? Is he pretending that he doesn't know me before he turns me in? Will they kill me?

The elevator opens, and I'm not at all prepared for what I see. There's color everywhere. So much color it's blinding. To the far right is a water slide that cascades into a swimming pool. Children are in there laughing and playing with beach balls. Right next to me is a bar with bottles of liquors and liqueurs of various colors. To the other side are women in barely there bikinis toasting under a heating lamp with fake sand surrounding their beach chairs. My mind reaches back to old ads of cruises and beaches.

I force myself to follow the man past the beach scene, wanting to stay and ogle at this paradise I haven't seen in years. Walking down a corridor with doors on each side, feet scuffle in a room and balls hit the walls. I glance in one, and four men are hitting a tennis ball with racquets against the wall. In another room, people use exercising equipment. I smell the interior room before we reach it. Sugar, salt, and grease mix together in the air. At the end of the hall is an open room with about a dozen tables and more chairs. In the middle of the room is a table with tiers of food I haven't seen in years: sausage, eggs benedict, biscuits, french toast, potatoes, pineapples and various tropical fruits.

Amazed, I watch a dozen people roam across this open room, chatting at tables and carrying on like there isn't a whole world collapsing outside.

"Which side do you want?" the man asks, knocking me out of my trance.

I look at him confused, and the annoyance grows on his face.

"I'll go there—" he points to one corner of the room. "You go over there." He points to the exact opposite corner.

I nod following his command. In the corner, most of the tables near me are empty except for one with a family of four: a dad, mom, son, and daughter. The kids both look to be under ten, well-fed and full of energy. The dad has a fresh haircut, and the mom's highlights look well-maintained. Although I don't mean to, I can't help but watch them in wonder. They eat as if all of this is normal, and they're just a regular family enjoying breakfast.

As the dad cuts into his eggs benedict with a fork, he asks the family, "What's everyone's plans for today?"

The mom replies, "Well Nancy told me the spa finally fixed the sauna so I'm going there for a few hours." She stretches her shoulders and rolls her neck. "I may need a shiatsu today. All that money we paid, you'd think they'd have better pillows."

The dad smiles a small smile. "How about you two?"

"I wanna watch Batman," the boy says, one foot out of the chair as if he's ready to speed off at any moment.

"I don't know if they're playing that today in the theater, son." He turns to the girl. "What about you, Emily?"

"Maybe I'll go with mom," she says, stirring her oatmeal with a spoon.

Massage? Spa? Theater? How big is this place?

As the dad continues speaking, a blonde lady enters my line of sight. "Excuse me." She waves a hand in my face.

"My slave is defective. I need a new one."

Her what? I struggle to hide the shock on my face in order to listen to her. She's walking as she's talking so I follow her. The shoes pinch my toes with each step.

"They brought him in yesterday, and when I told him that my robe was to be hand washed, he seemed like he didn't know what I was saying. He's either deaf, dense, or dumb."

"Yes ma'am," is all I can muster as she takes me further onto this floor. We pass the movie theater and the spa that the family talked about, and she leads me to another elevator. Getting in, she presses a few buttons and the elevator opens up to her room. It's more a suite with a large bed and windows that are a bright light with no view in them. I follow her to a closet where a frail main is curled into a ball.

"Here he is. I expect a new one by the end of the day."

She waits for me to act so I grab his arm, careful not to use too much strength and break him.

"Yes, ma'am," I say and drag the man to the elevator with me. I press the star button to return to the main floor, and when the door closes, I release him. He cowers into the corner.

"Please don't hurt me," he begs.

I leave him alone until the door opens, then I grab him again to keep up appearances. I drag him back down the hallway as he whimpers, and we return to the elevator leading to my room. I don't know where else to take him.

Once inside, I let him sit on the bed, and we stare at each other, trying to gauge the other's motives.

"What are you going to do to me?" he asks.

"Nothing," I admit.

"Why am I here? What is this place?"

"I don't know." I tell him, and his face shifts. Maybe he realizes that I'm not the authority figure he assumes I am. "What do you remember?"

"I was—" He looks at the floor, trying to remember. "I was in a house, looking for food and then these...these people showed up and beat me and I woke up in a room and then...they gave me some clothes, a little food, and said I had to work since I was looting. And that lady, she started yelling at me. Calling me dense and hitting me. And I tried hiding, but she just kept yelling and calling me her slave."

My back slides down the door as I sit on the floor. The FISCO soldiers capture scavengers and bring them here to be slaves? Who are the FISCO soldiers? They aren't like the people who expect others to serve them. Is this a job to them or are they as trapped as the scavengers are? And who are the people that live here like the revolution never happened? Why are they getting FISCO soldiers to capture and enslave scavengers?

The man watches me as I mull over the situation in my mind.

"What are you going to do to me?" he repeats.

"Nothing. You're free to stay here or leave."

I get up to return to my post. When I open the door, he asks, "That's it?"

"Yeah," I say.

I'm here to get as much as I can to save me and Chi. I can't save everybody.

When I return to my room, the man isn't there, but another tray of food is. I grab it and sit on the bed. It's pasta, salad, a roll, and a bottle of water. I twirl my fork in the warm pasta and bring it to my mouth. The smell of the sea fills my nose, and when I inspect the fork, I see the tiny bit of pink: shrimp. It would've killed me if I didn't double check.

Despite my stomach's grumblings, I put the fork back in the pasta, eat the salad with my fingers, chew the roll, and wash it down with the water. Then I set the tray outside before showering and sitting on the bed to massage my achy feet. I wonder about the woman here before. The real 4313. The woman whose shoes I can't fit. Why did she take this job? What was she doing? Did she have her own family to take care of? Guilt settles in my belly so I force myself to think about Chi. This is all to give us a fighting chance. We can survive well here. It's that thought that helps me sleep.

The next morning, I dress for the field and press every button in the elevator until I return to the floor from the day I got here. I fall in line with a group and join them in the back of a tank. They talk about how many scavengers they caught the day before and their fights in the field. It seems the more scavengers you bring in, the more you're rewarded. Like an extra meal, the chance to watch a movie, or have a drink at the bar. I don't care about any of that. I have to get Chi.

The tank stops, and the door opens up to a mountain of a man. "Two of you. Go," he commands.

Scanning the area, I don't see anything familiar so I stay as two women hop out of the tank. It takes three more stops until I recognize a couple of familiar landmarks and volunteer to search. A man joins me. After a few minutes of walking, he asks, "Why don't we check that house?" He points to a red brick house with a decaying roof.

"There's a scavenger settlement up ahead," I offer, unsure of how much information to give him without him seeming suspicious.

He's suspicious anyway, squinting his eyes at my sugges-tion, but he follows along. The apartments are about a twenty minute walk from the main highway and are surrounded by trees. It's difficult to find if you don't know what you're looking for. It's what's kept me and Chi safe for the past year and some.

When we get to the apartments, I ask, "Do you want to split up or search together?"

He agrees to split up, and I'm relieved. Once I see him head in one direction, I run in the opposite one looking for Chi. At the apartment door, I knock our signature: three short, one long, three more short knocks.

"It's me, Chi," I whisper.

The door opens, and he squeezes me into his arms. I gag from the stench of him, but I'm happy he's safe. We both are.

I reach into my pockets and hand him the two apples I've been saving. He chomps through them both, eating the seeds and stem. When he finishes, the questions start.

"Where were you? What is going on? Did you figure out what FISCO is? Where did you get an apple from? I haven't seen one in so long. Did you cut your hair?"

When he stops for a breath, I raise my hand to quiet him.

"It's some kind of bunker. There are families there living like it's before the revolution. And the soldiers get scavengers and bring them there to be their slaves."

"Wait. What do you mean before the revolution? And slaves?"

"They have movies and a pool—"

"A pool?" His eyes widen. Before the revolution, we used to have a pool behind our house. When society collapsed, we lost everything, including our parents. We assumed everyone lost everything they owned, but apparently these people prepared for the collapse and prepared to remain comfortable throughout. They were one step ahead.

"Yes, a pool. And they have so much food, Chi. Hot, greasy, sweet food."

"Who are these people, Gada? Do you think they're billionaires?"

We were told that the billionaires left Earth back in the twenties to live on another planet.

"Maybe not billionaires. Maybe millionaires."

He nods, taking this all in. "Did you come back to get me?"

"For what?"

"To join you? To be a soldier?"

"Chi, I don't think that's safe."

"Is it any safer than being here?"

Is it any safer than fighting rats for food, not having clean running water, or electricity? I exhale.

"Fine, Chi, but we have to stick together."

He pumps his fist in the air. Although a knot of worry grows in my chest, at least I can watch Chi and know he's safe.

When we rendezvous with the other soldier, he has two scavengers. Chi and I sneak attack the soldier. It doesn't take much to overpower him considering we're superhuman and he's not.

Chi squeezes into the man's clothes, but unfortunately, we have to sacrifice one of the scavengers to avoid blowing our cover. When we return to the truck, the mountain man takes the scavenger and scrunches his nose at the stink of her. He says that she's going in a separate transport. Guilt flops around in my stomach, but I look over to Chi who's staring at his hands in his laps. He's safe. That's all that matters.

Once we return to base, I lead Chi to my room where he showers for an extremely long time. He's smiling when he opens the bathroom door, and steam rushes out. The elation of cleanliness is clear on his face. It makes you feel like a real human.

He settles at the edge of the bed, and I use the clippers to cut his hair. He jumps when I press the button, and I smile at our mirrored reactions. When I finish, we sit beside each other, giddy with satisfaction. After three years of misery, we're finally returning to normal.

There's a knock on the door, and we both stare at each other. Unease grows. I motion for Chi to hide in the bathroom, as I get up to open the door a bit. Two men, a thin one in a suit and a bulky one in tactical gear, are at the door.

"4313?" the man asks.

I nod.

"May we come in?"

I open the door to allow them through. There's barely enough room for all three of us to stand there so I sit. The man in tactical gear has a bowl in his hands that I can smell the cheese and garlic emanating from it.

"I'll cut straight to the point." The thin man pulls out a tablet and shows me the screen. It's a video of my door. "Yesterday you were ordered to dispatch and replace a scavenger and instead of doing that, you released him."

The screen shows the man from yesterday leaving this room, looking from side to side, before running away.

"We got a complaint from Mrs. Tuttle when her new worker hadn't arrived, so I checked your record. Everything was clear except for three days ago, the food was returned uneaten. Then the strangest thing happened—" He looks at me and my jaw clenches as I'm putting the pieces together. I'm one step behind. Why did I think I could infiltrate a bunker and get away with it? Why did I think I wouldn't get caught?

"The pasta was returned uneaten which is strange considering we had all our agents fill out intake forms, and 4313 said her favorite food was shrimp alfredo. So that left me with two theories: maybe our chefs aren't up to your standards, or—and this is the likely bet—you don't belong here."

I gulp.

"Just by looking at you, I'm going to assume that you're a superhuman so we have to get...creative in how we dispose of you, or you can clear your name and just eat the pasta. Maybe it is the chef's fault."

He motions to the bulky man who uncovers the bowl and unveils the pasta. The smell of the sea, cream, and garlic floats near my nose. I close my eyes to the scent, and my heart quivers in my chest. This man probably knows Chi is in the bathroom, but I hope he doesn't come out. Maybe they can strike a deal with Chi. He's still young. Maybe they won't kill him. I hope Chi knows that I did everything I could to protect him and keep him alive. But I can't fight both of these men and fight my way out of here. I can't survive their torture. After all the fighting, I failed.

"We're waiting," the thin man interrupts my thoughts.

I inhale, grab the fork from the man, and twirl a bite of pasta. I eat it, chewing it slowly, savoring the butter and garlic, before swallowing. Within minutes, my throat swells, and I claw at it, wheezing.

The thin man's lips curl into a smile. "I thought so."

Tears stream from my eyes as I pray that my sacrifices and protection were enough to keep him safe. My lids swell shut. Heaviness descends on my body, but my last hope is that Chi survives.

Race Play

KIANA, 2015

When we met, the first thing Lucas asked was, "Do I know you? You seem familiar." And I could say the same thing about him—all blond waves and blue eyes. I knew it was meant to be so I sought out an old seer, Simone. In a reading, she confirmed that Lucas was my twin flame—our souls were tied to each other in a past life. Soul ties were karmic lessons, cycles we're bound to repeat or complete. She hesitated to call it love, but it had to be. How could I meet the same man in two different lifetimes if it wasn't a true love connection?

The only problem was that Lucas bored me every time we "made love." He was too gentle, too worried about my feelings, about if I liked it. All his kissing and thrusting wasn't enough to make me feel present, to make me feel much at all. I rarely craved violence, but with him it was necessary. I could only feel his love when pushed to its extreme.

We eased into it, progressing slowly. I initiated it by asking him to choke me during sex, first with his hands, then with a belt. When he felt comfortable enough with that, I asked him to handcuff me. The handcuffs were too loose so I bought rope and had him tie me to the headboard. Eventually we progressed to whips. We started with a leather flogger. It only tickled my back—barely enough to get off on. Next was the leather braided snake whip and finally a four foot bullwhip, the thread tightly interwoven to create the perfect sizzle once it hits flesh.

When Lucas cracked the bullwhip, my back reared up. The immediate sting reverberated throughout my body. My welts stood at attention.

"Harder," I commanded. My eyes were covered, but I squeezed them shut anyway, delighting in the pain. If he hit me hard enough, I orgasmed.

He cracked the whip again, and it split the air. The birds silenced. Blood rose, its metallic odor filled my nose. Snot and tears stuck to my face, and my hands were bound in front of me but around a tree. Bark scratched my cheek and chest as I pushed into it. He hit me again, and I slumped. Piss and shit ran down my legs. He stopped.

"Cut her down! Clean her up!" he commanded.

Feet scurried to untie me, to lift me. Fear forced my lids closed. Teetering between pain and pleasure, my burning back was the sole reminder that I was alive. That Joseph hadn't killed me yet. I was grateful.

In this lifetime I was a seventeen year old girl named Rachel in love with Joseph Miller.

They carried me up to my room. Hands hurry to apply warm water to my wounds. I hissed when the cloth stuck to the lifted edges of my back and whimpered when Ms. Harriet applied her salve and dressed the gashes. They cleaned the rest of my body and dressed me in loose linen before lifting me onto the bed. As the women scrubbed my blood from the floor, his heavy boots traveled up the stairs. He opened the door.

"You're dismissed," he said to the women who scurried out.

Laying on my stomach, it hurt to lift my head to see him. His thick wavy blond hair. The bright blue of his eyes. His angled jaw. He walked over to the bed, gently lifted my head, and rested it on his thigh. He caressed my face. The coolness of his fingers was the only reprieve to the burning flesh on my back. It amazed me—the hills and valleys of this man—someone who inflicted so much pain yet held me so tenderly. I sobbed into his lap.

"Shhh now," he whispered, his voice much cooler than the tight, booming one from an hour ago. "I went easy on you."

He did. I knew it, but it didn't hurt any less. I whimpered, and he shushed me again. His cool fingers grazed my arms. The smell of mint, basil, and blood wafted from my back.

"You gave me no choice, Rachel. You disobeyed me in front of them. I can't have anyone thinking I accept insubordination. Not even from you."

The insubordination was that he didn't want me to talk to any males on the farm, and Henry asked me if I could take over for Ellen in the wash house. We both got the lash, and my body still trembled from the shock of it.

"I only whip you cause I love you," he said.

"I know," I managed between tears.

"You'll heal, and everything will be fine."

He stayed with me until I fell asleep and then retired to his own bedroom. It took a fortnight for the wounds to start scabbing over. He checked on me every morning and every night, making sure I ate and that my wounds were cleaned and redressed.

On the morning of the fifteenth day, I sat up when he joined me in the bed and told him outright, "I want you to free me."

The laugh he gave was dark and hollow. "You know I can't do that."

Joseph was eighteen now. It was well within his power to free slaves. He could do it if he wanted.

"But you love me."

His hand cupped my cheek as he met my gaze. He smiled softly. I smiled back.

"I do love you which is why it's best you stay here with me. Where I can protect you."

"You can protect me even when I'm free."

"How do I know you won't leave me, Rachel? I can't take that chance. I need you here. With me." Irritation rose in his voice. He was done talking about this subject.

I stared at the foot of the bed. He didn't trust that I'd love him if I was free, but I would. I wanted the way we were here in the bed at night to be how we were outside in the daylight. If I was freed, then we'd be free to love openly.

His hand slid under the cover between my thighs. He massaged there and hovered over me. "I missed you," he whispered in my ears.

I sunk into the bed, protesting. My wounds were no longer raw, but they were still tender.

"You won't deny me," he growled. His hands clasped my throat, lightly at first, but then with a tighter grip.

I squeezed my eyes shut and kicked the covers.

"No! No! No!"

My shoulders were pinned down. "Hey! Hey! Safe word?"

I opened my eyes, and Lucas was there. The same wavy blond hair, blue eyes, and angled jaw.

I nodded and whimpered.

"Okay, you're safe." He stopped, wrapped me in his arms, and shushed me. Rocking while holding me, he patted down my hair and kissed my temple. "You're safe. I'm here."

I was safe in a lifetime where I was a twenty-five year old named Kiana dating Lucas. We'd been together for over a year. At least in this lifetime, Lucas didn't own me. I was free to choose him and him, me. He respected my no. I consented to the lash. We could live a life that wasn't allowed in 1850's America. We could have the love that we knew we deserved.

The only problem with Lucas was that there was no hunger in him—not the way it was with Joseph. They may be the same soul, but society molded them differently. Joseph took advantage of the power afforded him; Lucas was afraid to. So Simone showed me a way to travel back and forth between the two to help us uncover why the tie was created.

"Sex is a portal," she said. "Pain is the easiest way to travel through it."

Whenever Joseph took it too far, Lucas was there to reel me back in. I had a good system, I thought, until Lucas asked to meet me for an early dinner.

"I can't do it anymore." His head was buried and all I could see was the top of his waves. "I feel like a terrible person when I touch you like that."

I was so careful to ease him into it so it wouldn't scare him, and here he was trying to run away.

"You're not a terrible person," I placed my hand on his to reassure him, but he snatched it back.

"Kiana, the thoughts I have about you when I—" He shook his head. "No one should think that way about someone they love."

I could channel Rachel's body and thoughts temporarily. Could Lucas channel Joseph's too? We were different manifestations of the same soul. It's possible. Although we pretended, did Lucas only see a master and his slave?

"Lucas, look at me," I waited until he lifted his head. His blue eyes were sorrowful. "You are the kindest person I know. We can stop using whips if you want."

"No." His lips drew into a line. "A good person wouldn't treat you like that. Maybe it's best if I leave."

So he left. I wanted to protest, but I couldn't. Maybe something was wrong with me to have such a taste for violence that I sought it out. That I asked someone who loved me to treat me terribly. The gentle lull of love bored me, but the fiery intensity of fear? Orgasmic. Maybe this desire was why I failed spectacularly at keeping this man in my life. Who knew if I'd get a third chance?

RACHEL, 1855

Joseph built me a cabin as both an apology for the whipping last month and to deny the rumor he was soft on slaves. The townspeople heard that a slave slept in the house in a bed instead of on the floor. The cabin rectified that. Like before, only the other female slaves could visit me. Joseph sold Henry a couple of weeks ago for the question he asked me. His mom and younger siblings still call me a wench for it, to let me know that they resented the favor that Joseph showed me.

I was a traitor in their eyes. Sure, the master may have his pick of property, but I was to hate it, not enjoy it, and I was *never* supposed to call it love. I ought to be ashamed and cause I wasn't, I was even more of a disgrace. Joseph was all I had, though. My mother was sold away years ago. My father and siblings, I never knew. Joseph's parents recently succumbed to consumption. Orphans both, we only had each other.

But I was tired of living in the in-between space—more than a slave, but less than the mistress of the house—so I asked for freedom once again. His body laid over me. His seed spilled between my thighs. I smoothed my hands over the waves in his hair as he laid on my chest and waited for his breath to slow.

"Will you marry me?" I whispered, caressing his head.

He didn't speak for a long time, so long I thought he either didn't hear me, or he fell asleep.

"I can't do that," he muttered after a while.

"Joseph, you can."

"Negros and whites can't marry."

Maybe not officially, but we heard of the slaves who were treated as mistresses, paraded around on their master's arms, dressed in fine clothing and jewels. It was rare—the masters outcasted—but it happened.

He lifted up from my chest with a stony glare. "I give you everything you could want."

Maybe as a slave, but as a woman? As his lover? Don't I deserve more than to be kept a nighttime secret? A disgrace?

"We're not talking about this again." He rose from the bed, stormed across the dirt floor, and out the cabin.

And we didn't. A month later, he gathered all thirteen of his slaves into the parlor to introduce us to Miss Ann.

"She's to be my wife here shortly," he told us.

I stared at her with her blonde ringlets, starched green dress, and blue eyes. Like a doll set, the two of them were made for each other. Someone he could hold hands with in the sunlight. Who looked the way love was supposed to look for someone like Joseph.

I ran away from the group, hid under the oak tree in the back, and wept. Maybe I loved the way Joseph hurt me. He was an expert at that. But my love for him mixed with my fear of him and turned into something solid and sharp in my body. Something addictive and painful. I still longed for him. I may always.

"I didn't dismiss you. I should whip you again for insubordination," he said, minutes later. He stood by the tree with his hands behind his back. His future wife was probably with her chaperone.

"Joseph why are you—"

"Master Miller," he corrected me.

I nodded. The realization blinded me. I asked for more and was punished with the reminder of my place. Worse than the in-between space, I was back on the bottom. He had all the power, and he never shied away from wielding it.

"My apologies, Master Miller. It won't happen again." I stood, looking at the tree root to avoid his sharp face. "May I be dismissed?"

He scoffed and recited the scripture, "*When I was a child, I spake as a child, I understood as a child, I thought as a child: but when I became a man, I put away childish things.*"

Was that all I was to him? A childish thing? A game of pretend? Practice for his future wife?

"Do you understand, Rachel?"

I wiped the worthless tear from my eye. My head still bowed, I answered, "Yes, sir."

"You're dismissed."

I understood perfectly. He had everything he wanted. When he married, I was bound to be even more of a prisoner—split between a lustful master and a resentful mistress. There was no escape.

In this life I was powerless to free myself, but I could hold onto him for an eternity so he'd remember who he really was. He was the kind of man who took and took and never cared if he left enough to live on so now it'd be my turn to take. We would be bound in this lifetime and the next and maybe another one after that. If he wasn't gonna let me go, neither would I. *He* will never be able to escape *me*.

Antenna

I

Just go and pretend to be a person.

I sigh in front of the vanity. Candace will be here any second. It's just a small gathering, she told me, but even small gatherings drain my energy, especially when they're full of un-knowables. Who are these people? How do I talk to them? What will they think of me?

As I rub tinted moisturizer onto my face, Candace knocks on the bathroom door. I see her reflection in the mirror.

"Ready yet?" she asks, leaning against the door frame. Her curls are pinned away from her face, and she's wearing a fitted jogging suit. I look down at the pajamas I've worn all day.

"Do I look ready?" I turn my attention back to the mirror, take the scarf off of my hair, and start undoing my week old twists.

She stares at me a second longer before leaving the threshold. A minute later, I hear Mom laughing with her in the kitchen. I sigh. I haven't heard Mom laugh in months. As much as I need to get out of the house, she needs company, too. She needs to laugh.

When I finish my hair, I slip on a dress and slides and meet Candace in the kitchen. She kisses Mom on the cheek. "See you later, Auntie."

Mom squeezes Candace's arms. "You girls have fun tonight. Don't get into too much trouble, you hear?"

"Yes ma'am," I say and follow Candace out the front door.

The light is bright. A little too bright for late evening so I shield my eyes with my hand while Candace walks next to me.

"Are...you...excited for tonight?" She drags the words out, afraid of how I'll take them.

"I'm ready to get it over with."

"Money," she groans. "Don't be like that. It's gonna be fun. You been holed up in that house for how long?"

Six months. Since the day of my diagnosis. I don't answer her. Instead, I pick at my fingernails and gaze down at the pavement.

"Listen." She stops and puts her hand on my shoulder. "Tonight is gonna be super chill and laid back. For one night, forget all about your suadmira."

Easier said than done. I wish the suadmira would forget about me.

"Imagine spending twenty-five years of your life thinking something is terribly wrong with you because you can't do anything right only to find out it's your brain's fault, and there's nothing you can do to fix it." I exhale. "It's both my greatest relief and my worst fear."

"Well," Candace tightens her lips. "That sounds depressing so don't bring that up tonight. Instead think about the fun. The high. It'll be great. Trust me."

We walk the eight blocks in silence until we reach a small fenced-in house.

"This is Chet's," Candace says, widening her arms to showcase the house.

"Chet?" I raise my eyebrow. That's a...name.

"He's a friend." She shrugs.

"Who all is gonna be at this get together?" I should've asked this before I left the house, but alas here we are.

"Oh, just you, me, Chet, Jason, and Kwame."

"All boys?" I stand outside the fence, watching her unlatch it and walk up to the door. Kwame I know. The rest? Not so much.

"They're cool." She turns around and yanks my arm to follow her. When we get to the door, she knocks then rings the doorbell. After a few seconds, a tall, sandy blond guy answers the door.

"Candace." His mouth widens into a grin, and he squeezes her with his eyes shut. A friend? I hold my arm and shift my feet, uncomfortable with how long these two have been holding each other. I clear my throat, thankful that it's enough to tear the two apart. "You must be Money?"

"It's Monice, actually." Only Candace calls me Money. When we were younger, she couldn't say "Monice;" she said "mo-ny" like "pony" and eventually she changed it to "Money."

"'It's Monice actually,'" he parrots me. "You sound like one of those baby robots."

"Like the children's dolls? The one where you pull the string?"

"Yeah." He snaps his fingers. "That's it."

I hum. It's now—with his droopy gaze on me—that I see the whites around his hazel eyes are reddened.

"You're the one with suadmira, right?"

"Chet!" Candace smacks his arm.

"I am." I smush my lips into a smile, wishing this interaction will end soon, wishing I never left the house in the first place.

"That's cool." He hovers over me. "Did you know that that billionaire guy has suadmira? Anders Day?"

I *love* how often people will bring up famous people with my condition. I'm well aware that it exists in others, and that a lot of celebrities have it too.

"No, I didn't know that."

I did, in fact, know that, but I'll let him have his moment in the sun. He shrugs, then opens the space between him and the door. Finally, we're no longer his hostages. I follow Candace into the living room where Kwame, and I assume, Jason are sitting. Kwame rushes to embrace me.

"Long time no see," he whispers near my ear. When he pulls away, I see that he's cut his hair since the last time I've seen him and swapped his nose stud for a ring.

"You changed your ring."

"Yeah." He flicks it. The guy from the couch joins him and interlocks arms. "And this is Jason—my boyfriend."

"That's new." I smile. With the way Chet was holding onto Candace, I'm starting to feel like a fifth wheel which again makes me wish I would've stayed home.

"Come." Kwame grabs my hand and leads me to the couch. We sit facing each other so our knees touch. "I haven't seen you since you quit. What have you been up to?"

"Just—" I tap my fingers on my knee. How can I say sleeping and daydreaming without sounding like a bum? "Nothing really."

His brow furrows, obviously displeased with my response. "Can I ask about the—" he pauses, letting the silence finish the question. "What even is it? All I know is that it's some rich people's disease."

Everybody wants answers for what's wrong with me, but I'm not even sure myself.

"Well," I begin to explain. "It's not just rich people, obviously. It's daydreaming and 'psychosis.'" I air quote the word because I hate it. It makes me feel like what's in my brain is unreliable. Faulty. But it doesn't feel that way most of the time.

"And there are the little things like trouble eating, problems with light and sounds, lack of spatial awareness. Stuff like that," I shrug.

Kwame sighs and shakes his head. "But you can still get high with us tonight?"

"I would love nothing more than that."

***

The softness settles around my limbs. My palms rub the rough tweed of the couch. I lay in Kwame's lap while his fingers gently graze the bridge of my nose. Despite the heaviness growing in my lids, I gaze at the ceiling fan, and my sight blurs. It's coming.

Suadmira means being in my head 24/7. It can be beautiful and wonderful and useful when I want to paint the images I see. But mostly, it's exhausting. I often lose my grip on reality. It's why it's often so hard to feel and interact with others. Because I'm there—in the world I can only see in my head—I'm rarely here. But being high, I can feel everything all at once. It reminds me that I have a body. That I belong here on Earth having my nose tickled by Kwame. Feeling the warmth and tingle of his touch.

"You doing okay?" Candace hovers over the couch, blocking my view of the ceiling fan.

I smile then nod. I'm doing better than okay.

"Okay let me know if the dose is too high."

It's too late for that. I'm along for the ride. She squeezes my arm before leaving me on the couch with Kwame. I breathe in and out, waiting, watching, anticipating.

Chet sits on the coffee table. I only know because Kwame turns his attention away from me and towards him. When I turn my head, he's on his phone.

"Did you guys know that forty percent of the population has a voice in their head?" he asks.

He's just full of fun facts.

"It's kinda scary don't you think?" Kwame says. "That so many people can't think for themselves?"

"I don't know about *thinking*. It's a voice. When you think, do you hear a voice? Is it yours or is it different?"

I don't answer. Suadmira means I'm already seen as the odd one out, especially with my "auditory hallucinations," but the voice in my head sounds mature, feminine, and strong. Apparently, I sound like a child's doll, robotic, so the two voices are different.

"I don't know, man. I guess it's the same," Kwame answers.

"Money?" Chet asks.

"Monice," I correct him again. I twist my lips before replying, "I guess it's like what Kwame says. It's the same."

Chet leans back and stares at us. "So you're saying you hear voices?"

"I don't hear voices. I have thoughts," Kwame defends himself. "You don't?"

Chet stares at him, processing the insult Kwame threw before he shakes his head. "I think! I'm a thinker, bro."

He rises from the table and storms out the room. Kwame chuckles and then leans closer to me to whisper. "I don't know what Candace sees in him."

"They're dating?" She didn't tell me about it, but then again I rarely answer my phone.

"*Close* friends. According to her."

Speaking of close friends, I ask, "Where's Jason?"

"Probably laying down somewhere. He's a lightweight. The first time he took one of these, he broke his nose."

"Oh my God," I rise up from the couch, but the heaviness of the high forces me back down.

Kwame presses my shoulder back into his lap. "Nothing to worry about if you just lay here."

He smiles, and I smile back. My eyelids now droop to the point where it only makes sense to close them so I do. Kwame hums, an old hymn I haven't heard in years, and I feel it in waves—first vibrating across my chest and then circling my limbs. I surrender to the sound, the vibrations, the release.

Colors swirl.

Brown. Green. Earth Colors. Silver mixed with sugar and rust.

The swirls in the road lead to the brown building. A black hill in the background. The grass green; sky gray.

Do you remember, Monice?

Of course, I remember. The recurring dream. About the place. Umista, I think? A place. A planet? I remember.

I open my eyes, and Jason is there. My legs in his lap. I reach to touch his face. It's soft. He leans into my palm.

"You doing okay?" he asks. "I broke my nose the first time I tried this."

"I heard." I lean up to look at Kwame, but he's gone.

"Yeah, I just got up too quickly and fainted. Broke my nose."

"Where's Kwame?"

He points behind him to the hallway. "He laid down about five minutes ago. You were out."

"I—" I try to sit up, but I feel my body becoming one with the couch. It won't budge. It's too heavy. Instead my body twitches.

Jason shushes me and presses my shoulder into the couch. He rubs my legs and waves of calm flood my body.

"This shouldn't be legal," I mumble before I'm back under.

A diamond with a tail.

A kite.

A constellation.

Signals embedded in symbols.

Antenna.

Analog was perfect. Perfect transmission.
Repeat. Reboot. Reprogram.
We are antennas.
You're an antenna, Monice.

I gasp sitting up from the couch. No Kwame or Jason. I look around, and Candace is leaning against the kitchen island with Chet towering over her. He sees me and walks towards me. Candace follows.

"Do you need anything? Water? Juice?" he offers.

My mouth opens, but it's too dry to form words. I nod. My head spins as I try to figure it out. I'm an antenna. What does that mean? The constellation looked so familiar. It all did, but it's just the drugs, or my brain reintroducing things I've already seen on TV or the Internet. It could be the suadmira mixing with the drugs to cause wild hallucinations, but why do I feel like I *know* it?

Candace slides beside me when Chet hands me the cup of water. I sip it and shiver.

"Blanket?" I ask.

Chet rushes to his storage closet and brings back a fluffy throw. I send a weak smile in his direction. Candace wraps her arms around me and rubs my shoulders.

"You doing okay?" she asks again.

"How do you take this every night?"

"It helps me sleep," she shrugs.

"Do you...have lucid dreams?"

"It's weird. I have no dreams. I take it. Go to sleep. Then wake up. It's amazing." She squeezes my shoulders. "This is just the first hour. You have another hour to go."

"Another hour?" It feels like I've lived a lifetime. I wrap the blanket tighter around me and lay in Candace's lap. A twitch takes over my foot. I usually suppress them, but this time I let it travel up my legs, to my hips, belly, chest, arms, and now my whole body is wiggling.

"Are you cold?" she asks.

"Nope, just twitchy." I yawn and then I'm out again.

The next morning, the scent of warm vanilla wakes me. I slept on the couch all night, evident by the stiffness in my joints, so I'm slow to rise. A glass of water sits on the coffee table, and the condensation on it signals that it was left for me recently so I drink, embracing the relief of it moistening my parched throat.

"Mone—Monice." I turn and Chet's bringing me a plate of pancakes. "I made breakfast."

"Thanks," I say, grabbing the plate. "Where's Candace?"

"I left her in the bed. She's such a sleepyhead so I have to bring her breakfast." He leans on the back of the couch.

Left her in the bed? I squint my eyes, but smile. "She is."

"Syrup?" He asks, and I nod.

When he hands it to me, I eat my pancakes in silence—eating only half of them before my stomach starts feeling queasy. Although the most intense effects have worked their way through my system, some residue remains. My brain doesn't quite feel like it's mine again. It's like at any moment, I'll be back under the waves of the drug.

Everyone else slowly makes their way to the kitchen to eat. I scroll on my phone, waiting for Candace to wake up so we can walk back to my house together. When Kwame finishes eating, he joins me on the couch.

"How are you?" he asks.

I inhale, analyzing the tension in my body. "Still feel a bit groggy."

"You been drinking water?"

I lift the cup off the coffee table.

"And that's completely legal?" I ask him.

"You never seen the Terra-5 stores? They're everywhere," he chuckles. "It's very legal."

Terra-5. It would've helped to have known what I took before I took it. I curl my knees into my chest. "What's it like? For you?"

He tilts his head to the side and hums. "It's like...floating in the ocean. The waves gently rocking you back and forth." He exhales. Content.

"That's it?"

"Is there anything else?"

I bite my lip, wondering if maybe I should tell Kwame what I saw, what I felt, but maybe he'll dismiss it as a reaction with my suadmira. It could be just that.

"No," I lie. "It's similar for me, as well."

He squeezes my knee. "We should catch up. I've missed you since you left the agency. You wanna get lunch with us after this?"

I'll need at least a day to recuperate from whatever this is.

"How about brunch tomorrow?" I counter-offer, and he accepts.

Both him and Jason hug me before they leave me alone on the couch waiting for Candace to untangle herself from Chet. While I wait, I search the Internet for "Terra-5." It's perfectly legal like Kwame says. It can ship right to your front door. Flipping through a few sites, I learn that unlike Terra-7 which is an outlawed plant, Terra-5 was created in a lab to produce a legal, milder high. Benefits include euphoria and relaxation and side effects are red eyes, dry mouth, trouble with coordination, and anxiety.

Maybe it's anxiety, the feeling left from my dreams, but I keep searching and find a site that wants to ban Terra-5. It claims that Terra-5 hasn't been analyzed by the Drug Testing and Potency Agency for safety, but also that some people experienced hallucinations while on the drug. So I was right. The constellation and colors. It could've been a hallucination, maybe amplified by the suadmira.

As I search for others who've had hallucinations from Terra-5, Candace finally emerges from a bedroom. She's in a dress and sandals. I don't ask where the change of clothes came from, but I let her know I'm ready to go.

"It was nice meeting you, Monice." Chet bear hugs me in the doorway. I pat his back, waiting for this interaction to be over.

"You too." I smile before turning away from his house.

When Candace latches the fence, I ask, "So you and Chet?"

She swings her arms and looks back at the house. "Yeah," she says, her voice soft and warm.

"He's...sweet." A bit of a himbo.

"He is, isn't he?" She grins.

Her words go in one ear and out the other as she gushes about him on the walk home. Mom sits in the living room watching TV when we walk in. I go straight to my room, shut the door, and fall into the covers. The last thing I hear are the muffled sounds of laughter.

When I wake, the constellation is bright in my mind. The clock reads a little after three. I hop up and sift through the mound of clothes on my closet floor. I know it's in here somewhere. Eventually, I find some paints, a few brushes, but no canvases. Where did I put them?

I search under my bed before I remember that I stored my art stuff in the garage. Mom tries to engage with me when I leave my room, but I'm on a mission. I want this constellation out of my brain and onto canvas so I rush past her and open the door to the garage.

On a shelf are my old paintings, some fresh canvases, acrylics, oil paints, and brushes. I grab the magenta, canary yellow, midnight blue, eggplant, and white paints. Pulling my easel from the corner of the garage, I set it up and place the canvas on it. Stepping back, I can clearly see the constellation superimposed on the canvas—like a transparent overlay. I scan the room for a makeshift palette and find an old paper plate on the floor.

The pinks and yellows are the faintest so I squeeze them on the plate and brush them lightly. Then, I layer on the blue and purple—blending until I get hints of green, blacks, and richer purples. When it's to my liking, I tap the brush in white, smear it on the plate, and dab it on the canvas, placing the galactic dust where I see it in my mind's overlay. The last step is to draw the constellation. Using a filbert brush, I tap it in the white and carefully place a dot where I see the stars. On the left, I place the top of the kite. Then over, the two sides at a slight diagonal before adding the bottom dot. I place four dots for the tail that curves upward slightly.

When I step back, I notice something within the diamond of the kite. A bit of the white mixed with purple and pink to form this perfect little sphere.

Umista?

I shake the thought away. My overactive imagination is always trying to connect the dots. With the image out of me, I breathe a little easier. I clean the brushes in the bathroom sink, smoothing my fingers over the bristles to get the paint out.

"You doing okay?" Mom asks, and I jump. "Sorry didn't mean to scare you. You passed out in your room."

"I was tired." I watch the colors run down the drain.

"You painting again?" I hear the excitement she's trying to bury in her voice. I haven't painted in months.

"Yeah." I turn the water off.

"Okay," she pauses. "I'm gonna make dinner here soon."

I nod and start drying the brushes one by one with a hand towel. She leaves the threshold, and I'm able to finish cleaning in peace. I return the paint and brushes to the storage box and place the easel back in the corner before laying down in my room. I grab my phone, unlock it, and see the search results for hallucinations and Terra-5. It was what I searched for this morning before Candace was ready to go home.

I click on a forum of people who wrote about their bad reactions with the drug. It's the expected: vomiting, fainting, hospitalization. Nothing unusual until one user talked about the colors filling their brain. The sights and sounds. Fragments. I click on their profile and search through their comments. Except for this one, most are about cartoons and conventions. It's a dead end.

I sigh holding my phone, something about this experience was off. Sure, it could've been the suadmira, but I felt like it was more. Earlier, I saw that it hasn't approved testing. Why would it be sold in stores then? I search for the makers of the drug and find a company: Ratone Pharmaceuticals. It's a relatively new company, founded five years ago, but it only makes Terra-5. Who created Ratone Pharmaceuticals? I find an unknown man from South Africa. He's not it. Companies like these tend to have investors so I search for them and find a slew of names. None that sound familiar until I see one, the founder of Saturn Global: Anders Day. It can't be a coincidence that his name has popped up twice in the last twenty-four hours.

When I search "Anders Day and Terra-5," absolutely nothing comes up. It wasn't that hard for me to make the connection, but why does an investor not want their name to come up with their investment? It could mean that he has so many that it would be overwhelming or that he doesn't trust the product. But if he doesn't trust Terra-5, why? The lack of product testing? He has suadmira too so maybe it affects him the same.

I search "suadmira and Terra-5" looking for some clue to why I experienced what I did last night. Instead of answers, I find article after article about how Terra-5 could be the cure to suadmira or at the very least a treatment. A treatment? Maybe for others, but not for me. Maybe that's why Anders Day invested in this product. Does he want to treat his suadmira?

I lay the questions to rest for the night and have dinner in my room. Before I sleep, I set an alarm. Kwame wants to meet at the brunch spot downtown. I lay on my bed with my arms tucked on my sides and exhale. Am I really ready to go back into the real world?

II

Kwame sits outside the cafe with a mimosa in hand and shades covering his eyes when I walk up. He waves me over to sit across from him at the bistro table.

"I'm so glad you made it." He reaches his hand across the table, and I meet it.

"Me too." I look around and notice there's only two seats for us. "Is Jason coming?"

He waves away my question. "No honey, I'll see him tomorrow."

"Anyway," I lean across the bistro table. "How did you two meet?"

"He works at the agency." I squint because he didn't work there when I did. "He started five months ago," Kwame fills me in.

"Mixing business with pleasure," I tease.

"You're a fine one to talk."

I grin. I met Kwame three years ago when we both started working for McMillion Agency after college. He's a copywriter; I worked in graphic design. We quickly became friends—visiting each other's cubicles during the day and partying every night. Then there were the days where we brought the party to the office.

He sips his mimosa. "So you're doing okay, then? After Friday night?"

"Yeah," I say. My brain still feels weird, like the Terra-5 is up there clinging on for dear life.

"No weird side effects?" he asks.

I look at him. I know it's care and concern, but part of me still worries so I change the subject. "Did you know Anders Day funds Terra-5?"

"I didn't."

"It's supposed to be a treatment for suadmira."

He lifts his brow. "Do you feel...treated?"

I shake my head.

"Damn," he exhales. "I shouldn't be surprised. That man puts his money everywhere except in my pocket. Did you hear he's trying to find another livable planet? I don't know why, when he has the money to fix this one."

He takes another sip of his mimosa and then the waitress appears. I order water while Kwame requests a refill.

"I thought you could drink?" he asks.

"I can." I shrug. "Just don't want to."

"Do you want to talk about it?"

There it is. The reason I haven't left my house in the last six months. I tap my fingers against the table debating whether or not we need to revisit it.

"I—I get if you—if you don't want to," he stammers.

"No," I reassure him. "Maybe I do need to talk. It's just—it's all black for me."

One minute I was in the office, and the next, I was in the psychiatric ward. I blacked out and had an episode of psychosis. That's what the doctors said when I became somewhat lucid. After a month of observation, they diagnosed me with suadmira.

"You were fine one minute and then the next you were going on about stars and signs, jumping on tables. You said 'It's all connected.' And when anyone would get close to you, you'd start swinging. I thought maybe it was the flowers you took, but I'd never seen you like that."

I wince hearing him recount the story. The waitress comes back with my water, and to shoo her away, I order one of the first things that sound half-appetizing: salmon croquette with grits. Kwame orders then watches her walk away before continuing.

"You were going on and on about Amistax or something. You don't remember any of that?"

Do you remember, Monice?

The voice from my trip returns, but I blink it away.

"Umista?" I ask.

He snaps his fingers. "That sounds about right. So you do remember?"

I shake my head. "I don't. Umista was this dream I used to have when I was little."

His mouth flattens, and he exhales. "Damn. Well, I was here. You could've talked to me about it. Let me know that you were okay."

"I was embarrassed," I say softly.

Before Friday, that was the last time I saw Kwame, and I don't even remember it. I hate that's how he remembers me. It wasn't easy waking up sedated in a psych ward, not knowing where you are or why you're there, not being able to leave, not having any sense of comfort or safety. Everything that I had worked for my entire life vanished overnight, and when I was released from the ward, I was too embarrassed to go back to work, too embarrassed to find another job. I didn't know how a new job would accept my new diagnosis so I moved out of the apartment with Candace and back in with Mom. I can't think of a greater failure.

A tear tickles the corner of my eye. I blink, letting it slides down my cheek. Kwame reaches across the table to grab my hand and place it within his. He peers into my eyes. "You never have to be embarrassed with me."

"It was really bad, Kwame." My voice cracks.

"You've had worse moments. Remember when you were wallowing in a pool of your own vomit in the Fenian's bathroom because you were passed up on that promotion?"

I choke. Now *that* was embarrassing, especially considering I got promoted six months later.

"That was truly the lowest of lows," he says with a grin.

I smile. He's the first person that's made suadmira feel like it's not that big of a deal. Like it's not the worst thing that's happened to me.

"Thank you."

"Of course," He pats my hand. Looking past me, his eyes widen. "There's the waitress with our food."

He lifts his fork and knife in anticipation for his waffle. We eat. I can only finish half of my food before the taste sours in my mouth. I sip the water to cleanse my palette. Kwame foots the bill then offers to walk me back to the bus station. When we exit the patio area and return to the sidewalk; it's quiet. Being Sunday, the streets are bare—with a few stragglers here and there. The air around us is light, warm. I shove my hands in my jumpsuit's pockets, taking in the day. Feeling everything—the light, the wind, the ground—and nothing—no sweetness or warmth inside. Empty. Hollow. A vessel.

We reach the bus stop. I lean against the plastic barrier and thank Kwame for walking me.

"Do you want to have brunch again next week?" he asks.

"Yes." I nod. "I'd like that."

We hug. His wide palm rubs across my back in broad strokes. It's soothing. Bits of the tension I've been holding in melt away. He waves me off and walks back towards the parking garage. I lean my head against the barrier, closing my eyes to the sun, and sigh. I hear it then, a buzz in my ear. I swat at it, expecting a fly or a bee, but there's nothing. The buzz increases with a rhythm. My chest jumps with the beat, pulling me closer to the sound. Soon my whole body is tingling, itching, fighting to find out what it is I'm hearing.

I leave the bus stop and keep walking, letting my ears guide me. The closer I get to the sound, the less my heart pounds against my chest, like it's answering a call. I wander off the main sidewalk and down another street. The music is getting louder, eventually, I turn, and it's a wide open green space. A platform sits in the middle with a crowd gathered around. It almost looks like a black hill. I've seen it before, but I don't remember where. There's a sign before I cross the street that says: *FREE CONCERT IN THE PARK.*

I join the crowd. The band plays music that I can only describe as psychedelic. Stringed instruments. I can barely hear the words, just the notes being strummed, and my body grows heavy. My head tilts back, and my limbs wobble at my side. I close my eyes, unable to fight the limpness overtaking my body and let it move to the music. Let it sway. I'm lost in notes and sounds and rhythms. They thrum inside my body.

I feel.

I'm stuck in that loop for what feels like forever. It's when the band finishes their set and thanks the audience that I'm finally free. I look around at everyone else, eagerly watching the stage or chatting with each other. How long was I out? Were they out with me?

While gazing at the stage, wondering what's happening, a voice speaks next to me.

"You like these guys?" she asks, her voice soft and faint. She's petite in shorts, a bikini top, and a flower headband.

"No," I tell her. "I've never heard of them before."

She gasps, pulling her phone out of her back pocket to search something. When she finds it, she shows me the screen. "It's from their latest album. You'll love it."

I seize the phone. Their album cover is a picture of a clear blue sky with a small kite flying. The kite is yellow with red bows, but looking closer the bows are placed at each point of the kite, and there are four down the tail of a kite. I tilt the phone sideways and realize the bows are in the same spot as the stars are in the constellation I painted yesterday.

"What's the name of the album?" I ask the stranger.

"It's *Umista*."

Signals embedded in symbols.

You said "It's all connected."

I hand the phone back to the girl. "Thank you," I say, rushing back to the bus stop to go home. Maybe it *is* all connected. Why would I feel called to go to a concert and learn about a band that has the same title as the place in my dream?

When I get home, I rush to my room, shut the door, and boot my desktop. My fingers frantically type "Umista" into the search bar. "Umista album" is the recommended suggestion, so I click it. The titles of the songs are all new-agey: Divine Feminine, Soul Ties, and Manifestation. Nothing of particular use to me. I glance at the album cover again. The kite is a symbol, but for what?

I search for "kite signals" and find information for how kites can signal certain things. How about "constellation signals"? There are a few search results that seem promising. I click on a video short where a shaggy brunet guy asks, "You ever wonder what humans used to think the constellations meant?"

A slideshow of pictures of the night sky covers the screen as the guy voices over it: "Early humans believed that constellations were created by the gods who lived among the stars. Some saw constellations as roadmaps to other planets. Many ancient civilizations believed that the constantly shifting stars told a story. Whether it's Orion with the Greeks or Osiris with the Egyptians, these stories told the history of humans battling against forces so great it was memorialized among the stars. Now we know that constellations had practical purposes for agriculture and navigation."

His pale face returns as he looks into the camera and says, "What have y'all heard about constellations? Let me know in the comments."

The video loops, and I pause it to scroll through the comments. Most of those in the comments battle about which constellation theory is actually correct. The trolls remind people that these are theories and not facts. Scrolling, I see one user comment: *The roadmap makes sense if you consider the human antenna theory.*

The human antenna theory? I search for it, and a number of videos show up. I click on a twenty minute video where the woman opens sounding more like she's telling a ghost story than a conspiracy theory. Annoying, but I power through. She starts by talking about when she was first introduced to the concept. She explains antenna like we don't understand what it is so I skip through until she gets to the meat of the video. It takes about seven minutes. The video stills, and there's a title: *Origin*.

The woman speaks again in her ghost story voice. "It all started with aliens," she pauses for dramatic effect. "Aliens came to our planet from another planet or maybe a few different planets. I always wondered if it was Mars because it used to have water which means it used to have life so maybe when they destroyed their planet, they came here, but now are they here to destroy our planet?"

The screen jump cuts before she continues, "In order to survive here, they had to breed with humans and create a human-alien hybrid. Some called them 'starseeds' or 'indigo children,' but as you may suspect, the hybrids were not very successful. Many of them died, but there were a few who survived. It's believed that they could find each other through signals—"

My ears perk up when she says that.

"—that allow them to recognize each other. Because of this, they're called antennas. Were they named after antennas or were antennas named after them?" Another jump-cut. "They say human antennas can still transmit and receive signals with each other today. Who knows why? Maybe it's their plan to take over the world. Maybe they're trying to get back home. Maybe they want to repopulate Earth with all alien-human hybrids."

As she continues to muse, I hover over the screen and see there's another six minutes of the video so I click off of it. Scrolling through the other human antenna theory thumbnails, they seem to suggest the same things. There are humans today, descended from aliens, who can send signals to each other. Sure, it's just a theory, but what if there's some truth to it?

I rub my tired eyes but continue to search for "human alien hybrid" hoping to get a fuller grasp of this concept. Instead of conspiracy theories and spiritual content, the feed is filled with fear-fueled titles like *Reptilian Aliens Take Over the Government*, *Aliens Poison Water to Turn Frogs Gay*, and *Alien Race Mind Controlling Citizens*. There's a lot of guns and so much green blood in the thumbnails.

Wording can really change the reception of an idea, but I find a video that attempts to sort through the noise of human-alien conspiracy theories. It's an hour. I groan but settle in. The video chapters include an introduction, unidentified flying objects, abductions, underwater creatures, alien-human hybrids, and more.

Yawning, I click on the hybrid chapter and watch the clips of extremists sharing their views on aliens. One, a thin blonde haired lady believes that aliens have infiltrated the government in order to make humans their slaves and that their fight against the government is really an intergalactic one. A brown-skinned man with wrinkles around his eyes yells loudly about how billionaires are aliens who rape children and drink their blood to appease their celestial gods. A balding man with a bad tan squints into the camera and talks about an alien gene that appears in humans and how their goal should be to find it and eliminate it. All three of them are quick to demonize what they don't understand.

The documentarian's voice returns, and he weighs each of these claims refuting them all. Despite the spiritualists, conspiracy theorists, and extremists all having the same pieces, they are drawing completely different conclusions. Part of me wonders if somewhere within these polarities is the truth.

I lean back against my computer chair—my brain, dizzied, from the plethora of information thrown at me. That trip the other night at Chet's felt like a puzzle and the more I dug, the more sense it made, but also that sense is uncertain. If I'm correct, the constellation I keep seeing is a road map to Umista. And if that's the case, I'm a descendant of an alien species who I don't think wants to drink the blood of children or overtake the government, but who can be sure? I blacked out at work. What if others like me black out and do horrible things like that? What does this all mean? Who am I?

I drag myself from the chair to the bed and lay there. Taking it all in. What's real? I wonder before I close my eyes and fall victim to my exhaustion.

III

When I wake up my first thought is of the web of conspiracies. It feels like this is stuff I shouldn't know, stuff that's too dangerous to know, but all the pieces were there waiting for me to put them together. It was hidden in plain sight. If conspiracy theorists can get online and talk about it, and they don't go missing, I'm fine, right? Maybe I'm fine. Maybe it's just my suadmira causing me to see and think things that aren't really there.

I turn to see the sticky notes and trash laying around my desk from my research frenzy last night. My brain doesn't feel as foggy as it has the past few days, like the Terra-5 has finally worked its way out of my system, and my thoughts are clear. Mine. I feel reset.

Rolling out of bed, I start grabbing the notes with words scrambled on them: human antenna theory, alien gene, constellation roadmap. All garbage. When my trash can fills, I grab a bag from the kitchen and start throwing away everything. The empty water bottles on my nightstand. The chip bags and candy wrappers on the floor. I pick my clothes up and shove them in my laundry basket. I grab my sheets off the bed, put them in the washer, and start it.

Walking back to my room, I pull back the curtain and squint from the brightness of the morning light. I lift the window to let it air out the room. To let it air me out.

In the kitchen, Mom left breakfast before she went to work. I eat slowly before dressing to bike around the neighborhood. I bike gingerly, taking in the color. It's early spring. When I moved back into Mom's, everything was dying, but now bougainvilleas are in full bloom, flowing across fences. The blues of hyacinths and purples of primroses stun. I turn down a street and am greeted by the bright yellows of forsythias and dark violets of pansies. Colors so bright and stunning, they swirl before me with an intense vibrancy that leaves me dizzy. I stop.

When I look up, I see that I'm out of the residential district and am now in the business sector. I hop off my bike, walking with it. Looking ahead, the shops bustle with office workers getting coffee and delivery workers dropping off packages. On the opposite side is a big brown building that I'm sure I've seen before. Behind it, a green hill.

The buzzing from the day before returns. This is a signal. A place I should be. I leave my bike outside. A bit upset I forgot to bring my lock, I enter anyway. The entire inside of the room is an off-white color, cream. A woman around my age sits behind a wide mahogany desk. Her hair is pulled back into a bun, and she's wearing a suit. She smiles when she sees me. As I walk closer to her, she asks, "Are you here for the Umista Project?"

She couldn't have said what I thought she did.

"The what?"

"The Umista Project. That's what you're here for, right?"

"Yes," I answer, hoping that she doesn't realize I'm lying.

She smiles and points toward the door behind her on the left. "Great, you can wait in there. Someone will be in shortly."

"Thanks," I mumble and walk into the left door. It's a conference room with a long table and ten chairs. Four on either side and two at the head. I sit at one of the head chairs and wait, pulling out my phone to search for "Umista project."

There are no results.

My palms sweat. I don't know what I just signed up for. As I'm thinking about leaving, another woman walks in. This one with a blonde blowout and a black pencil dress.

"I'm glad you got my messages, Monice."

What messages? And how does she know my name? I never gave it to the woman at the front desk. I'm about to ask her when I realize that I know her voice. I've heard it somewhere. Mature. Feminine. Strong. My eyes widen when I recognize it, but she simply smiles.

We have a lot to discuss.

When her mouth doesn't move, I stammer, "What? Why are—how are you?"

"Is this better?" she verbally asks.

I nod, confused, trying to figure it out all. She's the voice that I've always heard in my head. So I *have* been hearing voices.

"Do you want me to start?" she asks, sitting at the other end of the conference table. "I'm Bobbi. You're an antenna. Suadmira is what humans call the expression of our alien gene. It doesn't always show up. For example, your mom and Candace don't have the gene. Your father did."

My mouth opens and closes, trying to form a question, but I can't put into words what I want to say. She slides me a hefty military green folder. In it are my birth certificate, a photo of my ID, medical records, pictures that I thought only my mom had of me in the family photo album. They even have a photo of me at Dad's funeral when I was eight.

"How do you—"

"Signals," Bobbi answers. "That's how you got here today. Do you understand how they work?"

Barely.

"When I'm near a signal, my body vibrates or something, but I don't know how it happens," I answer.

"Signals are how we send and receive messages. Some call it telepathy, but we can share images and thoughts with our minds. There is a limit though. Antennas have a certain range that we cover. A few decades ago, we used analog to spread that range. Two antennas could spread signals across the whole country but now? I'm the main antenna for the state."

"That...must be a lot of people."

"Antennas only pop up in about one percent of the population. Unfortunately, only thirty percent of antennas are useful to us. The useful ones follow our network of signals and end up in the highest positions on the globe: astronomy, law, government, medicine, music, art"—she gives me a pointed look—"That constellation you keep painting, it's a road map to Umista."

How does she know about what I've been painting?

"We know a lot of things."

I frown at her, realizing that she just read my mind...or picked up my signal?

"Honey, you're wide open right now. But okay"—she raises her hand surrendering— "I'll ignore your thoughts. For now."

She tilts her head to study me and see how I'm processing everything she's thrown at me so far. It's a lot, but I can tell that she has more to say, more answers that I want to know.

"Let's take a step back, shall we? You took the Terra-5 and—"

My head rises. I knew something was off about that drug. "What the hell is in that?"

She chuckles. "As I said earlier, our range was strongest with analog. Digital interferes with our signal. It makes it harder for us to communicate. Have you ever noticed the brain fog when you're on your phone or computer for a long time? Do you feel wiped out from looking at screens? That's why. We developed Terra-5 as an activation drug. It cuts through the noise and makes you more receptive to signals. We tell people it's a cure for suadmira, and they line up at our door." She shakes her head in disbelief.

I sigh knowing that since I've been diagnosed, I haven't been desperate for a cure, just desperate for others not to point out how different I am. I've had suadmira—or been an antenna—my entire life. I've learned to adapt with it, but it's everyone else who can't seem to accept me. Why can't they sit in the uncertainty of the unknown?

She clasps her hands in front of her. "Do you have any questions?"

I lean my head on my hand, trying to sort through the millions of questions running through my brain. "Why are you telling me this?"

"You're one of us. You have a right to this information, and it's important you know that we're not a threat. We come in peace." She makes a V with her four fingers and smiles. I'm pretty sure those are two separate alien references, but okay.

"If you have all this information about me. Why didn't you say anything sooner? You could've let me know that something was wrong with me years ago."

She sighs. "First, nothing's wrong with you. Believe that. Second, we believe in choices. I can only send you so much information, but even as a child you knew something was different about yourself. Everyone around you knew, too, I bet. They would point out your every 'flaw.' I'm sure you drowned yourself in drugs and alcohol trying to fit in. The story is similar for most antennas. It was your choice to ignore the signals, and you have been up until recently. But, you followed them, and they led you here. You want answers so I'm telling you."

"So," I say, trying to wrap my head around all of this, "I am a descendant of an alien species. That mated with humans to create a hybrid to survive on Earth. We have a gene that tends to be passed on from antenna to antenna, and it allows us to share thoughts and images. Although it seems that you're the one picking up everything I think—"

"We can teach you how to control what you share," she offers, but I wave it away to finish my train of thought.

"But we share signals, and it's a vast system of signals in every area of the globe, and you've been trying to activate antennas now with Terra-5 because of what? Umista?"

"Yes. The Umista Project started ten thousand years ago although it had a different name. Our home planet was destroyed, and our only hope for survival was a new planet. Earth was the nearest habitable planet for light years so we weren't the first intergalactic species to end up here though—"

"Wait, so there are other aliens?" This is much bigger than I thought.

"Yes," Bobbi replies. "The Earth is...crowded. But not all aliens are humanoids. Some are fauna or flora. When we are hybrids, humans are quite adept at identifying us. Unfortunately, they say we are mentally ill. Psychotic. You understand."

Unfortunately, I do.

"Anyway," she continues. "Our goal ever since we got to Earth was to integrate to survive—and when we had the re-sources—to leave. Our network of signals ensures that our kind is able to gather as many resources as possible."

"So is that why so many billionaires have suadmira? Like Anders Day?"

"Day," she exhales deeply. "We prefer to work in secret, but unfortunately Day has exposed more than we care to share with the general public which is why his name is often associated with suadmira and space programs, much to our chagrin. Thankfully, humans are very quick to dismiss what's right in front of them."

I cross my arms on the table and bite my lip, putting everything together. "So you hoard resources from humans and just let them suffer?"

I think back to all of the extremists who claimed the alien invasion had already happened. Were they right?

Bobbi sighs, "Unfortunately, we have to do what it takes to survive. As everyone knows, this planet is quickly becoming inhospitable. The ocean levels are rising. The globe is heating, and the coasts are eroding. A zombie virus is ravaging Europe and Asia and is headed to the US next. If this continues, human life will cease to exist in the next few centuries. With the technology humans have, it'd take them thousands of years to travel to Umista, but with our resources, it'll take us about a century. We are recruiting antennas for the trip to...breed while aboard," she swallows. "While you and your children won't see Umista, you can ensure that your lineage survives."

I blink then exhale. She wants me to give up my life to create antennas and die in space?

"What if I say no to this project? Are you gonna kill me?"

She grins. "Of course not. You're one of us. You have the right to say no. As I said earlier, we believe in choices, but you do realize that staying here means facing extinction? The human race will be wiped out. I know this is a difficult decision, but it's the same one our ancestors made thousands of years ago when they came to Earth. Are you going to waste their sacrifice or honor it?" She pauses for me to ingest the question, then continues. "We can't promise that your descendant's body will adjust well to Umista. We're still mostly human after all, but it likely won't be much different than the way your body responds now. It is a risk, but staying here is riskier."

"How am I supposed to explain all this to my mom? About going to another planet?"

"Sweetheart, do you really think anybody will believe you?"

My shoulders sink. They'll claim it's psychosis. Say I'm having hallucinations. They'll pathologize what they don't understand.

"How about this? The first ship leaves at the end of the year. If you give me your decision by then, I can have you on the second ship next year. Take your time to decide, Monice. You know how to reach me." She taps her index and middle finger against her temple, rises from her chair, and leaves the room.

The air is heavy with the decisions that Bobbi left on the table. I drag myself out the door and to my bike to tread back towards the residential district. I gaze at the houses filled with people who don't know the truth of how the world works. How right, wrong, and oblivious we all are.

What do I really have here? I don't have a job. I've never been in a meaningful relationship. Nothing is really tying me down. Mom pities me. Candace doesn't want me telling her how suadmira—or being an antenna—affects me. Kwame is the only one who makes me feel okay, but he has Jason. Who do I have?

If I stay, I'll forever be an alien. Forever the odd one out. Not fully accepted for who I am. Umista is a century away. I will never see it, but I can ensure that my descendants do. That they have a chance at a normal life, but what does normal even mean? I've never known it. It's a pipe dream at this point.

I walk past the flowers that I rushed through earlier, past the houses that have been a mainstay my entire life. This morning, the world was brimming with color and possibility. Now, that the world—or the hope of another one—is at my feet, I don't know what to do. I don't know what choice to make. Although far from perfect, this is the only life I've ever known.

When I pull up to the house, Mom's car is there. A burst of air conditioning greets me when I open the door. Maybe my brain senses how safe I feel because now the heaviness of the day settles in my body. Mom sits on the couch watching TV. Her graying hair is pushed back into a puff. I sit beside her and notice the wrinkles around her eyes and mouth. For so long all we've had is each other, and who knows how much longer I'll have her.

I squeeze her. "I'm so sorry Mom. I locked myself in my room and didn't talk to you and I've just been a mess and not good at anything in my life and I know you hate how much of a failure I am and—"

She shushes me and rubs my back. "Monice," she whispers softly. I rise from her chest, and she wipes the tears that've streaked my face. "You are not a failure. Everyone needs a little time to sort themselves out."

"But I've done nothing for the past six months."

She waves her hand to dismiss my concern and wraps her arm around me. "Look at you now. You're going out with your friends again. You're painting. You even cleaned up that room of yours." I chuckle, then she continues. "You're going back out in the world, and what did you find?"

The truth.

The Town of Los Valles

In loving memory of Ramon Figueroa

As we turned the final corner, The Hills came into view. The Hills was a luxury community filled with stunning white houses that had terracotta-tiled roofs. Each one competed with the last. The vibrant and spacious green lawns. The arched windows of Mediterranean revival homes. As the shuttle driver pulled up to our rental, I saw that the house we were staying in had a balcony on the second floor. Me, Mom, and Gabrielle grabbed our suitcases and walked up the side staircase into the house.

Walking in, we saw the kitchen with two stoves and a bar, the living room that opened into the balcony, and the dining room in the back. Gabrielle sat on the gray couch and put one of the orange pillows under her head. "It looks like one of those HGTV homes."

"It's a three bed, two bath," Mom said, scrolling on her phone, looking at the original listing for details. She scanned the room and then back at the door. "If we came up the steps, maybe the rooms are downstairs?"

We walked through the dining room and found the stairs down to the first floor. The three rooms and one of the bathrooms were accessible from the middle hallway which led to the back door. I went through it and saw the pool, grill, and lounge area. "There's a pool!" I called to Mom and Gabrielle.

"I'm jumping in that right now," Gabrielle said.

We took our suitcases and went to our rooms to change. Gabrielle found a bottle of wine in the fridge and carried three glasses with her to the side of the pool.

"Three?" I asked her.

"One for you." She twisted the screw into the cork and popped it out. "You just graduated from high school. You deserve a toast."

"What about Mom?"

"I got your mom." She winked and poured into each of the three glasses.

"One of those for me?" Mom asked, walking out of the house in a bikini. She tied her sister locs into a bun.

"Mom! Where are your clothes?"

"This is my hot girl summer, okay?"

"Excuse me? I'm pretty sure hot girl summers are for the single ladies which you are not," Gabrielle said, reaching her arm around Mom's waist.

"I'm still a hot girl."

"That you are," Gabrielle said, kissing her on the lips.

I cleared my throat. "Your child is here."

"You're eighteen, my dear. You will live," Mom said, grabbing one of the glasses of wine. Gabrielle handed me the other glass which incited a glare from Mom.

"She's eighteen, right?"

"Fine, she can have half of this." Mom poured half of my cup into hers and handed the glass back to me. "Cheers to my baby who finished school and is on her way to USC." She raised her glass in the air.

"Cheers!" Our glasses clinked with hers.

"And cheers to Black girls looking fine and living in luxury," Gabrielle added.

I giggled. "Cheers."

While we were talking in the pool, a little boy with rosy cheeks walked out the door. "Who are you?" he asked.

Mom got out of the pool, wrapped a towel around her waist, and approached the little boy. "Honey, are you lost?" she asked, placing her hand on his shoulder.

"No," he stared at her. "This is my house. Why are you here?"

Mom looked back at us. We shrugged. The boy lifted his head to the door to yell for his mother. A tall thin brunette woman emerged, and once she saw us, clutched her son. "You need to leave. Immediately."

"I'm sure this is just a misunderstanding—" Mom tried to reason.

"No," Gabrielle cut her off, coming out of the pool. "We booked this place for the weekend. It seems like *you* need to leave."

"That's impossible." She reached for her phone in her back pocket and dialed a number eyeing us. "Hello, Carol. There are people on the property. They *claim*—" she put heavy emphasis on the claim, like we were lying— "that they have the house for the weekend." She listened to Carol on the other side. "Well, are you nearby? Should I call the police?"

Mom and Gabrielle looked at each other. Mom's jaw tightened.

"Okay, I'll see you soon." She turned her attention back to us. "The property manager will be here to sort everything out."

When Carol arrived, she donned a royal blue velour tracksuit. Although at least sixty years old, she tried to hide it with a face lift, fillers, and botox injections. She brought a folder and a police officer with her. Scanning the folder, Carol told us, "It seems that we're double booked for the weekend. Usually, we'll try and place you in another house, but since it's the holiday weekend, everything's full. I'm so sorry about this, but the Reynold's have first claim to the house since they booked first."

"But we were here first," Gabrielle protested. "So you're kicking us out?"

She nodded, "I'm really sorry about that." The slight smirk on her face as she said it showed us that she wasn't really sorry. "We can offer you a refund. Officer Vasquez can escort you to the nearest town. Hopefully you can find a place to stay there." She turned to Officer Vasquez. "Can you escort these ladies and their things out?"

He followed us to our rooms. I pressed the towel into my swimsuit trying to dry it as much as I could before slipping on a dress. Once my suitcase was packed, I rolled it over to Mom's room where her and Gabrielle were aggressively whispering to each other. Officer Vasquez stood next to the door. I sat on the bed when Carol peeked her head in.

"I found this empty bottle by the pool. I'll have to deduct that from your refund." She smiled, taking pleasure in our suffering.

Mom breathed a heavy sigh, and anger burned in Gabrielle's eyes. Officer Vasquez sensed their frustration. "It's best to comply," he offered softly.

Betrayal flashed across Gabrielle's face, but they kept packing.

"I'll talk to Carol and see if you can't get a full refund." Although he didn't have an accent, I could tell from the way he moved his mouth when he spoke that he could speak Spanish. My Spanish teacher often scolded us for mumbling, claiming that perfect Spanish pronunciation required us to open wide. That we'd always be able to know a fluent Spanish speaker by how wide they opened their mouths when they spoke English.

Officer Vasquez followed us to his SUV, even offering to put our suitcases in the back of the truck. I looked out the window and watched the sprawling white houses that were once inviting turn into spurned towers. Through Mom's window, I saw the town below us. Unlike the white houses surrounded by gray rocks and green hills, the town was brown and bleak. Mom was on the phone doing whatever she could to salvage our vacation or get her money back. Once we got to the bottom of The Hills, the officer drove through town. The buildings were in disrepair—windows barred and marquees faded. He parked in front of the motel.

"I hope you ladies can find a place to stay," he said, offering a sympathetic smile.

"Thank you," Gabrielle said curtly, her jaw still clenched.

"So," Mom addressed us as we stood outside the motel. "I tried to get a Lyft from here to the airport and thought we'd stay at one of their hotels, but the price for the Lyft alone is ridiculous. The shuttle doesn't run on the weekends, and since Monday's a holiday, they're only running Monday morning. I moved our flight up from Monday night to Monday afternoon. So we have to find out where to sleep for the weekend," she sighed.

"I'm sorry, Mom," I said. I knew how hard she and Gabrielle worked for us to have this vacation.

"No, I'm sorry baby," she hugged me. "This was supposed to be a celebration for all of us and now," she sighed again. "Let's get a room"

We had to ring the bell a few times before a woman came to the front, her confusion apparent on her face. "Can I help you?"

"Yes, we'd like a room." Mom gave a small smile.

"We're booked. No vacancies."

Gabrielle clutched her chest, like she was going to have a heart attack.

"Do you mean all weekend? Is nothing gonna open up? This afternoon or tomorrow? Please, can you look?" Mom asked.

The woman shook her head. "I'm sorry. It's the holiday. We're full."

Tears stung my eyes at the thought of being stranded. I choked and rushed out the door hoping the fresh air would provide relief. Opening the door, I accidentally hit someone. "I'm so sorry," I said, reaching for this stranger.

"It's okay." He held his nose. "It was my fault." He peered at my face, witnessing my distress. "Are you okay?"

"I'm fine." I tried to wave it off to this stranger, but then the anxiety of the day bubbled up in my chest and exposed my lie. I wiped my eyes. "I'm sorry. I don't know what's wrong with me."

He motioned for us to sit down on the bench near the sidewalk. I sat down and couldn't keep it in anymore. "I just...this was supposed to be a vacation, and we were all gonna celebrate and have fun and those people in The Hills were so mean to us, and they kicked us out and...and," I sniffled.

The thought of Carol smirking at us was seared in my brain and burned my chest.

"I'm sorry that happened to you." The guy leaned in and gently asked, "Did you say you were kicked out of The Hills?"

I nodded.

He shook his head in disbelief. "They do this shit all the time."

"They what?" I asked through my tears.

He rolled his eyes. "Yeah, they always calling the police to kick out people who are 'undesirable,'" he said the last part with air quotes. "Usually, we have room at the motel, but um, I know someone. She usually helps out in these kinds of situations."

"Really?"

"She has a BnB. I'm sure she'll let you stay. I can take you to her if you'd like," he offered.

Mom and Gabrielle walked out of the hotel. Seeing my tears, Mom rushed to my side and cradled my face in her hand. "Mom this is..." I looked to him for his name.

"I'm Rodrigo, ma'am," he told them. He got up and held his hand out to theirs. Mom took it suspiciously.

"Rodrigo. He said he'd help us."

Mom's eyes gave away her wariness, but we were out of options. We either had to trust this stranger or be stranded. "How?" she asked.

"I know someone who has a BnB. I'm sure she'd let you stay for a few nights."

"Why are you helping us?"

"It's what we do here," he shrugged and smiled.

"And where is 'here,' exactly?" Gabrielle asked.

"Where are my manners? Welcome to Los Valles." He spread his arms wide like he was presenting the town. "Let me show you around."

He led us down the street from the motel, and we walked westward on the sidewalk. I walked next to him while Mom and Gabrielle trailed behind us. Once the tears stopped, I could get a clearer look at Rodrigo's face. He seemed young, maybe nineteen or twenty. His nose was pierced with a stud, and his hair was cropped at his shoulder. He smelled like citrus and cedar.

"I didn't catch your name," he said.

"I'm Myiahnna."

"Like the Disney princess. Moana. Myiahnna." I liked the way my name danced on his tongue. "That's a pretty name."

"Thank you."

"And they are?"

I turned and pointed. "That's my mom Layla and my step-mom Gabrielle." I leaned closer to him to whisper. "They just got married a few months ago so they're still in that super gross newlywed phase." I rolled my eyes. He laughed a full body roar which was kinda cute. I bit my bottom lip to tamper my grin.

We walked for a few more blocks before we came across a two-story red house with an arched entryway. Rodrigo opened the latch to the fence and let us go ahead of him. He knocked on the door and a stocky brown skinned man answered the door.

"Necesito ver a Abuela. Tenemos invitadas," Rodrigo told him.

The man glanced at us and then shut the door. After a minute, he came back and let us in. We followed Rodrigo to the kitchen where a fat older woman sat counting a wad of cash. She had at least four stacks piled on the kitchen table.

"Rodrigo!" she said with a cigar hanging out of her mouth. Her accent was thick and gravely. "¿Qué pasa?"

He whispered something in her ear. Mom looked at me and mouthed "Drugs?" judging from the money on the table. Abuela nodded along to whatever Rodrigo was saying. When he finished talking to her, she gazed at us.

"You were kicked out of The Hills?" she asked.

"Yes ma'am. We were unpacked and another family came in and called the police on us," Mom explained. "The property manager claimed that they booked first so they had first rights to the house." A tear choked her words as she recounted the story. Gabrielle rubbed Mom's arm.

"Those people—" she pointed her cigar in the direction of The Hills— "are nasty people. I remember when they built that place. They just started throwing their trash all over town because that's how they see us: basura."

"That's horrible," Mom said.

"It's evil," Abuela corrected. "Now the people have trouble breathing and problems with their health." With every word she said, her chest rose in anger. She sighed, shook her head, then smiled at Mom. "But you don't have to worry about them anymore. You can stay with me."

"We can pay," Mom offered, fumbling through her purse.

"No need," Abuela smiled. "Their enemies are our friends. Rodrigo, take them up to their room."

Rodrigo led us upstairs to a room with a king size bed, dresser, chair, and a bathroom. "Unfortunately, you all have to share a bed," he said.

"This is perfect. Thank you," Mom told him.

Gabrielle walked over to him and whispered, still loud enough for us to hear, "So what kind of operation y'all have going on here?"

"Gabrielle!" Mom and I hissed at her.

"What? We were all thinking it!"

Rodrigo laughed. "It's not drugs. I promise. Most of the people here work in The Hills. We're the drivers, housekeepers, pool cleaners, cooks, whatever they hire us to be. None of us get paid enough for it so we—" he paused to measure our faces—"skim to survive."

"Wait, how?" Gabrielle asked.

"You know the funny thing about rich people. They're so worried about someone stealing their credit card while on vacation using some fancy machine that copies their info that they heard about on social media. They just walk around with wads of cash." He shook his head. "Easy targets."

"And you never feel guilty about stealing their money?" Mom asked.

"This country was founded on theft. We just playing the game."

Mom shrugged knowing she couldn't argue with that.

"I know I keep asking questions, but I gotta know. What y'all do with all that money?" Gabrielle asked.

"Nah, I get it." He smiled. "The money's for anyone that needs it. Food, bills, medicine. Whatever."

"So you got your own little Robin Hood operation going on?"

He laughed. "Yeah, something like that." He slapped the door on the way out. "I'll let you get settled. I'm gonna stick around a little longer," Rodrigo said and turned his gaze towards me. "Let me know if you need anything."

***

When I woke up the next morning, my eyes had crusted over, and my throat burned. A shower softened the crust around my eyes. Although I sometimes had seasonal allergies, they were never this bad. Brushing my teeth barely helped my sore throat then I got dressed. Mom was still asleep in the bed, snoring. Downstairs, Gabrielle was in the kitchen talking to Rodrigo.

"Good morning, Myiahnna," Rodrigo smiled, put his cup down, and walked towards me. "Are you hungry? I wanted to take you to get breakfast."

I glanced at Gabrielle, and Rodrigo followed my eyes. "I mean, if it's okay with your parents?"

"You're grown," Gabrielle said waving me towards the door.

I smiled at him. "Sure."

We walked the first block in silence before he asked me if I slept okay. I told him about how I must be allergic to the air.

"It's the pollution," he said.

"Is that what Abuela was talking about yesterday? About the trash?"

He nodded. "For the most part, you learn to live with it, but it's really bad in the morning."

We walked the same street the cop drove down the day before and passed an unoccupied gas station, botanica, and church. I got a closer look at the abandoned grocery store with bars on the window. Most of the shelves were bare inside. "Why are there so many abandoned buildings?"

"A lot of the same people who own those houses up there also own most of Los Valles. They raise the rent on these places to the point where no one can afford to rent them so they sit and rot. Because they look that way—"

"They can dump whatever they want here," I finished his sentence, understanding more about The Hills/Los Valles dynamic.

"Yeah. Because it's a shithole. It's a self-fulfilling prophecy."

I sighed. "That's messed up."

He nodded. We walked another block, and I read the signs of the buildings. Most were in Spanish. One building read: Iglesia Casa de Oración y Alabanza

"Church House of Prayer and Praise?" I translated it out loud.

Rodrigo's eyes followed mine to the sign I was peering at. "Hold up! ¿Hablas español?"

"Más o menos," I said, waving my hand back and forth.

He gasped and put his hand on his chest in shock. "Pero ¿me comprendes?"

"A little yeah. I'm better at reading it than speaking it."

He tucked his hair behind his ear and smiled at me. "You're full of surprises, huh?"

"I guess so," I smiled back at him.

He stopped in front of a house. "We're here."

"It's just someone's house."

"Sure, but this someone sells the best breakfast tacos in town. You'll love it."

Rodrigo introduced me to Señora Rosa who did in fact make the best breakfast tacos I ever had. She made mine without chorizo because I'm vegetarian, but the tacos had beans, eggs, and potatoes stuffed into a homemade corn tortilla. I added a little salsa verde to mine and had to catch myself when I licked my fingers after finishing the taco. Rodrigo let out a small laugh, and I was embarrassed at how publicly I enjoyed Señora Rosa's food. He paid her, and she kissed him on the cheek before sending us on our way.

"So how were the tacos?" he asked once we got outside.

"Best breakfast tacos in my life."

He pumped his fist. "Okay, but I'm not done showing you the best parts of this place. I have to work today, but you can ride with me." He eyed my outfit. "You'll need your bathing suit."

"For what?" I raised an eyebrow.

"We're going to the beach."

Back at the house, Mom was awake. I changed then she reminded me to keep my phone location on. Although Rodrigo and his family were friendly, they were still strangers.

I joined Rodrigo in his car, and he turned on the driving app heading up to The Hills. It was strange that just yesterday we were being evicted out of the so-called paradise and exposed to what's really going on behind the scenes. Once a request for the beach came in, Rodrigo took it. We parked at the end of the curb. The gardener tilted his hat to Rodrigo, and Rodrigo threw his fingers up to acknowledge him back.

The couple came out of the house. The girl had on a full face of makeup and a scantily clad clamshell white bikini. Her blonde hair was styled in perfect beach waves that she covered with a wide brim hat. Her skin tone was nearing the color of mine. The man was also tanned but not nearly as much as the woman. He was muscular, but his face looked like it could barely grow hair. I didn't think they could be any older than twenty-two maybe.

The girl tapped on my window. He let it down. "Rodrigo?" she asked.

"Yes, and you're Jessica?"

"This is it, babe," she told the man. They put their beach bags in the trunk and scooted into the back seat. "Do you know where we're going?" Jessica asked Rodrigo.

He peered at the app, "Um...La Joya Beach?" He pronounced the "J" like "Joh" instead of "Hoh." "It's twelve minutes away"

"That's the one," she chirped.

Rodrigo drove. Exiting The Hills, the Pacific coast came into full view. The morning sun sparkled on the deep blue water, and the sea stacks looked other-worldly. I couldn't believe that The Hills blocked this amazing view from Los Valles.

From the rearview mirror, I could see Jessica gaze in her compact mirror to fix her hair to her liking. "We have to get some good shots for this campaign," she told the man she's with. He grumbled. "They paid for this whole trip, and it's three thousand dollars for the promo."

"I know. I know," he sounded frustrated. "But are we gonna spend all day at the beach taking pictures and not going in the water?"

"It's my job." The annoyance in her voice was palpable.

I glanced at Rodrigo who gave me the same look: trouble in paradise.

"Hey everyone," her voice shifted to a rehearsed sing-song one. "Tanner and I are absolutely in love with our house in The Hills. Today's a beach day, and as you can see the water looks absolutely beautiful. I'm in a piece from Swim 2 Shell's summer collection. You can use my discount link in bio for twenty percent off your order."

The story audio looped in the car.

"Do you have to do that now?" Tanner whispered.

"Yes, I do." Her voice was tight. Once the audio stopped, she said, "It's done. Now we just have to get footage for this video, and you can swim or whatever."

As we were coming around a corner in the road, Rodrigo turned on his blinker and pulled into a parking spot. The app notified us that we had arrived. Rodrigo popped the truck, and Jessica and Tanner grabbed their stuff.

"Thanks for the ride, Roberto," Tanner said and handed him a twenty.

"Oh, no problem, Brian," Rodrigo said back to him. I tried to stifle my giggle.

Tanner stopped, confused. "It's um...Tanner, but you probably didn't know that. My bad."

"Have fun!" Rodrigo yelled out the window as he backed up and drove off.

"What happened to us going to the beach today?"

"We're not going to the tourist beach. There's a beach that only we know about," he said, smirking.

"Another secret of Los Valles?"

"You know it."

We drove for another two miles until the road became a dead end. Rodrigo parked. This beach was a bit more secluded. Besides us, there was only an older lady in a sunhat and a fanny pack who picked up trash along the shore. I took my shoes off and followed him onto the beach. The powdery sand cushioned my feet like memory foam. The salt from the ocean kissed my nose, and the waves created their own melody with the shore. He sat down about five feet from the shore line so I joined him. The faint smell of cedar and citrus wafted across my nose.

"Is every weekend like this for you?" I asked.

"What do you mean?"

"Taking people to the beach and coming out here to the ocean?"

He dug his big toe into the sand. "I wish. It's usually just dumping tons of Barbies and Kens at the beach and picking them up when they're drunk. They're always doing some social media thing." He exhaled. "You know, if you're quiet and don't even bother them, they treat you like you're background. Sometimes it's better that way."

With the way the people in The Hills acted, living in Los Valles seemed like more trouble than it was worth. Staring out at the ocean, I asked him, "Why don't you just leave?"

He put his hands in the sand behind him and leaned back. "It's, um, it's complicated. My family's been here for a long time. This is our home, you know? We can't just pack up and leave." He cleared his throat, stood up, and changed his tone. "We came here to have fun. Let's have fun. Do you know how to swim?"

"Um...," I hesitated.

"I'll take that as a 'No.' Don't worry. We'll stay in the shallow part." He winked.

He took off his tank top and used the ponytail holder from his wrist to tie his hair up into a bun. With his hair up, his face came into focus. I saw the glimmer in his eye and the cherub roundness of his cheeks. I followed his lead, stripping down into my swimsuit and quickly braiding my curly hair into two loose braids. He jumped in, swam out a few feet, and motioned for me to join him.

"It's not deep. I promise," he said.

I hesitantly got in the water. It was frigid, and I instantly regretted my earlier willingness. Slowly, I made my way to him.

"It's cold." The water only came up to my knees, but even that was too much.

"It takes some getting used to. You just gotta dunk yourself in." He pinched his nose with his fingers and gestured for me to follow his lead. When I did, he held his breath and nodded. We both plunged into the water. It rushed over my head before I emerged from it. Now my whole body was cold, but the ocean was less so.

"Better?" he asked.

"A little." I was still shaking from the temperature shock.

He rubbed my arms to try and warm them up. "Aww. I'm sorry. Let me show you something though." He spread his arm wide and laid back like he was doing a trust fall with the water. His body bobbed and weaved with the waves. "If you can't swim, you gotta learn how to float. It's the easiest thing. I can teach you." He flipped around and swam back to me. "You have to lay back and trust the water." One of his arms went under my back and the other under my knees.

"Spread your arms out."

I did.

"Tilt your head to the sun."

When I did so, the water lapped around my ears.

"Straighten out your body."

His hands guided my legs to straighten out.

"And breathe." He took a deep breath with me. "My arms are under you so don't worry. Just keep breathing."

I closed my eyes and kept breathing in through my nose and out through my mouth. The water flowed around me, and my body slowly stopped resisting the current. Instead, it flowed with the water, bobbing up and down like Rodrigo's had earlier. The warmth of the sun sparkled on my skin, and the saltwater breeze caressed my face.

"Just keep breathing," he coached.

I smiled and felt brave enough to open my eyes to peer up at him.

"You're doing really good," he smiled back at me. "See? No hands." He showed me his hands, and I started to panic. My arms flailed as I tried to regain my balance and stand up. Salt water shot up my nose, and when my feet touched the sandy bottom, I started coughing. He rubbed my back. "Are you okay?"

I nodded, struggling to breathe.

"It's okay," he reassured me. He moved the tendrils of hair that came undone out of my face and wiped the water away from my eyes. His hands were under my jaw, and his thumbs wiped away the rest of the water from my cheeks. All I could do was stare up at him, watch how his face glowed in the sun, and strands from his bun swayed in the breeze. Our eyes locked in mutual understanding. One of his hands dropped from my face and tightened around my waist. I tilted my face up to his. When we kissed, I could taste the saltwater on his lips.

"Anything else you wanted to show me in Los Valles?"

He held my face and smirked. "Oh, I think you already seen the best we have to offer."

***

The next morning over breakfast, Rodrigo invited us to a party. When we arrived that evening, it was a lot that was filled with picnic benches. Bistro lights and multi-colored flags hung in the air. There were a few red hot conical grills. The sweet scent of pineapple mixed with spiced pork wafted from one. From a distance, the officer from a few days earlier talked with Abuela. When he saw us, he waved before walking over. He was wearing plain clothes and holding a can of Tecate beer.

"Hi ladies, I wanted to apologize again for Carol. She's always calling us up there," Officer Vasquez rolled his eyes. "I talked to her. You should be getting a full refund."

"Already got it. Thank you for that," Mom said.

"And how has my baby brother been treating you? Showing you the best of Los Valles, I hope?" He wrapped his arm around Rodrigo's shoulders.

"Brother?" I mouthed to him. He gave an awkward smile.

"Rodrigo has been a great tour guide for us. Everyone's been so generous," Mom told him.

"They should. You're one of us now." He put his beer up in the air to cheer. When he saw that Mom and Gabrielle didn't have one, he said, "Let's get you two a drink."

"Yes, please," Gabrielle laughed.

They followed him while Rodrigo and I got food. We sat down, ate, and I asked him, "You're Officer Vasquez's brother?"

"Darwin? Yeah," he shrugged.

"So you're related to the whole town?"

"I told you my family's been here a long time."

We heard a shriek from the makeshift dance floor. Gabrielle dipped Mom, and both of them were howling about it. Rodrigo got up and motioned for me to join him. When I did, we swayed to the sound of the guitar. Mom, Gabrielle, and I twerked to the banging of the drums. Our bodies filled with joy and relief at every note. Once the violins came out, Rodrigo held his hand out for mine. Then he grabbed my lower back and pulled me closer to him. The smell of his cedar-citrus cologne filled the space between us. Past his head, I saw the orange, pink, and purple of the setting sun and smiled.

"Is that smile for me?" he asked.

I gazed into his soft brown eyes. "This has just been a beautiful weekend. Thanks to you."

"Maybe I should add 'tour guide' to my resume?"

I giggled. "Maybe you should." But then I thought about it. "Wait, does that mean you're gonna take every girl that ends up here to the beach?"

"Nah." He brought his hand up to cup my cheek. "That's just for you." He gulped and stared into my eyes. "I'm really glad I met you, Myiahnna."

"Me too."

His lips curved up into a smile. I pulled my face closer to his and kissed him.

"Myiahnna!" Mom's shock filled my peripheral vision.

Rodrigo chuckled, but I rolled my eyes. "Mom!"

"She's grown, Layla!" Gabrielle defended me.

She seized Mom who said, "My baby is kissing boys."

I buried my face in my hands while Rodrigo laughed. He clasped one of my hands, twirled me, and kept dancing. We danced until the last note was played.

The final morning, Rodrigo and Darwin walked us to the airport shuttle station. Everyone else shuffled ahead of us, while Rodrigo and I trailed behind, not wanting the vacation to be over. Despite my initial horror, I was charmed by this small town and the people in it who laughed, loved, and celebrated despite the atrocities surrounding them. I wasn't ready to say goodbye.

When Mom and Gabrielle rounded the corner, Rodrigo grabbed my waist out of their view. His breath was warm against my lips. "¿Un último beso?"

I pulled his face closer to mine and embraced the electricity of his kiss.

"Myiahnna!" Mom yelled. I rolled my eyes remembering last night's theatrics.

"I hope you enjoyed your vacation," he whispered.

"I did. Thanks to you." I grinned.

He clasped my hand and brought it up to his lips before we turned the corner to the shuttle stop. The shuttle pulled up to the station. "You're welcome back anytime," Darwin said, helping Mom and Gabrielle onto the bus.

Rodrigo held my cheek and rubbed it with his thumb. He kissed my forehead and said, "Nos vemos luego, Myiahnna."

In Los Valles, they don't say, "Goodbye"; they say, "See you later."

Acknowledgements

In the summer of 2020, I had a series of apocalyptic dreams. Dreams where Black people were murdered, and I was lynched by a trusted friend. Dreams where the rich survived societal collapse, and Black superheroes murdered the white supremacists who were attacking them. At the time, we were a few months into the global pandemic where Black people had the worst health outcomes and had learned of the deaths of Ahmaud Arbery, Breonna Taylor, George Floyd, Tony McDade, and Oluwatoyin Salau. Angry, frustrated, and grieving, I went to my altar daily crying about the injustices but felt powerless to do anything about it. In my prayers, I recognized that writing could be the way that I transmute the pain, fear, and anxiety into something useful. Into art. In July 2020, I wrote the first iteration of "Entangled" and set out to create a collection mirroring the horrors of everyday life.

These are my horror stories.

Thank you to my ancestors for your unwavering love and guidance. It is because of your support that I write and remain encouraged to share my stories.

This collection would not be possible without the Bereket Writing Community. Thank you Nicole Blum, Laura Ortega, and Sophie Song for your thorough feedback over many months to help me shape this collection. Thank you Sevde Kaldiroglu for inviting me to workshop my writing and be in community with other writers.

Thank you Danielle Buckingham, Herbert Girtly, Rachel Long, and Petra Lurch for being readers for at least one short story and encouraging me to create a collection. I know there was a lot of resistance on my part to create a speculative fiction collection, but I did it.

Thank you Bethany Hensel, Leah Pierre, and Natalie Obando for all of your support in the Authentic Voices Fellowship. Shoutout to the women I met in that program: Shipra Agarwal, Akanksha Aurora, Jae Carey, Jenna Mayzouni, Jenise Miller, and Shaina Nez. You've been invaluable to me as a sounding board and support system for my writing, especially Jenna!

Thank you William Atkinson, Anita DeRouen, Liz Egan, Kiese Laymon, Michael Pickard and all of my writing instructors who have encouraged me to constantly expand my idea of what a story can be and do.

Thank you Clydette deGroot and The deGroot Foundation. Winning the Courage to Write Grant was life-changing and affirming as a writer. It showed that not only did someone see my work, but they appreciated it enough to financially support it. Thank you Grubstreet Boston's Writers of Color as well for your Literary Support Stipend.

Thank you to *Samjoko Magazine* and *Sistories* for publishing versions of "Apocalypse, Still" and "The Pastor's Wife." Thank you Octavia Butler, Zora Neale Hurston, Dolores Kendrick, and Toni Morrison for the legacies you've left that helped to inspire this collection. To the women I haven't met but whose work I admire: Ismatu Gwendolyn, Ayandastood, and Tatianna Morales. Thank you for being the first or second person whose words inspired me to share this book with the world.

Thank you to my mama who shared her love of magic, witchcraft, and the supernatural with me. Although I tried hard to resist your nerdiness and love of fandoms, I fear I inherited it anyway. Thank you to my daddy for showing me the importance of stories that center Black people. We are main characters, too.

Finally, thank you, Reader. A reader is necessary to complete a work. This collection is merely a seed that I hope you plant, water, and grow. I hope you think about these stories, let them live on in you, and if you wish, expand them. I wanted to show the ways we harm, protect, and fail one another under the institutions of race, class, gender, sexuality, and ability, not to finger wag, but because I believe in us. In a country that has continuously failed us, all we have is each other, and we need each other if we intend to survive our current apocalypse. I hope we understand this before it's too late.

About the Author

Leah Nicole Whitcomb is a community storyteller from Mississippi who writes about Black folks, love, and magic. She co-hosts the award-winning Hoodoo Plant Mamas podcast. Her writing has been featured in *Sistories, Samjoko Magazine* and the young adult anthology, *All the Ways a Heart Burns*. A Courage to Write Grant recipient, Leah's work has been supported by The deGroot Foundation, Voices of Our Nation

Arts Foundation, The Bereket Writing Community, Women of Color Writers Podcast, and the Women's National Book Association. She is the author of the short story collection, *Apocalypse Still*, and the young adult romance series, *About the Boy*.